TaiLorMade Books Presents

Partially Broken Never Destroyed IV
Unholy Matrimony

By Nataisha T. Hill

Chapter 1

"The bachelor party is about to be off the chain, dog!" said Wayne in an over ecstatic tone.

"Look, Wayne, I told you I want something simple. I'm not trying to get mixed up in anything with these stripper hoes you mess with," responded Bryan, reaching in the refrigerator to grab him and Wayne two beers.

"Really Bryan? Is Mr. Saint judging women now? All strippers ain't hoes."

"The ones you fuck with are," Bryan said and laughed, sitting down at the kitchen island.

"Man…yeah, you're probably right," said Wayne, laughing with Bryan while answering his cell phone.

Bryan and Wayne had made amends with one another shortly after the hostage situation with Jennie and Raymond Jenson. Wayne said he had no idea that Ms. Jenson had ever dealt with Bryan. Jennie told Wayne that she was new in town, she happened to see a nice-looking man at her construction site, and she wanted to get to know someone new in town and Wayne seemed liked the type of guy who could show her a good time.

Although Bryan could have sworn he told Wayne about Jennie at some point, he decided to let the past remain in the past since he was marrying Kayla, the woman he truly loved.

Bryan had his focus and his attention strictly on business and his marriage. He was just as excited about the wedding as Kayla was. He was making more than enough money to support him and Kayla both, even though Kayla decided not to quit her position at the hospital. With both incomes coming in, they were able to buy a bigger two-story home in an extremely nice neighborhood.

Bryan's boss, Alex, didn't lose any business in regards to Ms. Jenson's shenanigans the year before. The contracts were already in place by Alex's dad, who was the real tycoon of the construction business, and his mutual business partners who obviously had a lot more pull in the business than Ms. Jenson. Once the business partners found out about the trial and Ms. Jenson's misconduct, they were unanimously able to vote her out their committee.

Bryan had been very accommodating to Kayla ever since the standoff between him, Kayla, Ms. Jenson, and Raymond, Ms. Jenson's son. Deep down inside he felt as if he was the reason that Kayla was held hostage, as she had to endure her son being locked in a closet, and watch Raymond torture and attempt to try to kill them. Normal people didn't experience a crazy predicament like that. Bryan felt that a part of Kayla would be scarred for life due to his negligence of sleeping around with a married woman. He made a conscious decision that from now on he was going to have his head on straight and discuss anything he felt he couldn't handle with his future wife.

"Yea, baby, just make a right at the corner and you'll see a big brick home with red, yellow, and pink perfectly trimmed bushes in the front and all that shit," explained Wayne, hanging up his phone.

"Man, don't be inviting none of your random bitches to the new crib, mane."

"Man, stop being so paranoid all the damn time. You should know me enough to know I wouldn't invite some jump-off to the new crib, besides, this is my future wife we're discussing, not a random side chick."

"Wayne, gone on somewhere with that bullshit you're talking about because you of all people know your ass can't be faithful," Bryan said and laughed. He was shocked because he had never heard Wayne even mention the possibility of marriage.

"That's what type of shit I'm talking about right there, Bryan. Why do you always feel like you're the only man in this world that can change his lifestyle?"

"No, what I said is YOU'RE not that dude. I don't know everyone else."

"Listen, dog, I'm on some serious shit. I'm really thinking about asking Jesse to marry me."

Bryan paused to see was Wayne joking or did he want some type of sincere reaction from him. The look in Wayne's eyes said he was serious, but how could he be serious when he was just bragging to Bryan about some chick he banged two weeks ago?

"Now Wayne, I'm no Einstein at this marriage shit, but I do know your not suppose to have sex with other women when you're exclusive with your woman."

"I wasn't married a week ago, Bryan, damn."

"What do you mean a week ago?" Bryan asked surprised. "You boned that girl again, Wayne?"

"Bryan, you of all people know I don't love those hoes. Jesse said it was her time of the month and then this other freaky bitch I had cut off continued to send me all these nude pictures and shit."

"Okay, so I doubt if Jesse will be going through menopause anytime soon, so what are you going to do when you're married and she's bleeding? It's all about getting into the practice of being with only her."

"What the hell is menopause?"

"Dude, it's when your woman don't bleed anymore."

"Well, you just fixed our problem. If she can stop the rag then we're good."

"You're not serious, are you?"

"About what?" asked Wayne, very confused.

"Forget it, dude. What I'm saying is if you keep acting single, then you will never get in a married state of mind. If you're really serious, man, you have to first cut off all ties with any other woman and change your damn number."

"That's genius! Look, B, this is where I need yo help. If you let Jesse and I hang around you and Kayla for a little while, then maybe it will help me pick up on some things I'm supposed to do, so I can learn about this inclusive thing."

"Wait, what? Don't you mean exclusive, dog?"

"Man, whatever. I'm about to go outside and wait on my baby, man, with yo judgmental ass."

Bryan shook his head as Wayne walked out the back door to go wait for Jesse. He knew Wayne had to really care about this girl to even entertain the idea of marriage. Wayne never met his mother, so he's always had intimacy issues. The tenderness and nurture that most moms provide were obvious things that were absent from his upbringing. Therefore, Bryan knew that Wayne didn't have a real concept of the emotions and feelings that women go through when they're hurt. He also knew that married or not, Wayne couldn't resist a nice ass and a cute face. He would definitely be the type of man to cheat on his wedding night if given the right woman and opportunity.

About ten minutes later, Jesse walked in the back door in short blue jeans shorts, a halter top, and matching wedges that accentuated her calf muscles. Her fluffy brown curls and brown eyes on her cute little button face definitely met Wayne's physical expectations. She was just as sexy back in the day when Bryan was smashing her as she was now. Bryan hoped that everything that happened back then would stay back then.

"Oh my gosh, Bryan, you're home is beautiful," Jesse exclaimed, moving around the kitchen and sitting at the island table.

"Thank you," he responded, leaning on the opposite end of the counter waiting for Wayne to walk in behind her.

"Where's Wayne bigheaded ass? He finally asked, circling back around to close the door.

"Oh, he's outside fixing some wires on the DVD player he installed in my car yesterday. He'll be in shortly, no worries. Are you uncomfortable around me or something?"

Bryan wasn't about to answer any slick or trick questions from this broad. He could feel something in the air from the way she was staring at him. He hadn't really seen her in a while since that one time she dropped lunch off for Wayne at work, but she couldn't keep her eyes off him. After Wayne walked off, he could have sworn she winked her eye at him.

"What are you guys about to get into?" He asked, totally ignoring her question.

"This kitchen island is really huge, Bryan. I'm sure you and your woman could make love on this thing all night," she added, also ignoring his question.

"What kind of subject is that?"

"The kind of subject where you pretend as if we didn't have great sex back in college."

"What?" he asked, completely thrown off by her answer.

At that awkward moment, Wayne came through the door with his beer still in his hand.

"Okay babe, I got you all fixed up," he said, walking over to Jesse and kissing her on the forehead.

"Baby, before you walked in, Bryan was asking when were we finally going to get a home together," Jesse said.

"No the hell I didn't," Bryan quickly responded, frowning at her deceitful antics.

"Oh, come on Bryan, it's like that, man? You know we've been living in that crowded apartment too long now. Don't you think it's about time we made some grown and sexy moves?"

Bryan looked at her and then turned his attention back to Wayne. He wanted to bust her out so bad, but how could he? Wayne adored this girl for some odd reason and would probably believe whatever she said anyway. It would also mean him admitting to the past affair he had behind his friend's back. Besides, Wayne still had his whorish ways, so clearly neither of them was truly committed. Bryan knew he was deeply in love with Kayla, so why entertain petty gestures from a woman he didn't want.

"Hey man, you two do what's best for you. You don't need my opinion. My guy, we have to go and meet with Alex, let's roll."

Wayne walked Jesse to her car and gave her a long kiss before jumping in Bryan's Hummer. He turned around and blew her another kiss before she pulled out of the driveway.

"I'm telling you, Bryan, I think I really can change for this girl. She's pretty as hell, she has no kids, a good job, and did you see how thick that booty was, dog?"

"Wayne, there's more to a woman than a pretty face, thick booty, and a good job."

"I know that, Mr. Perfect, but what I'm saying is that I feel different about her. She says things I can actually relate to and she's always finding the positive side of something even when I think it's a no win situation."

"Wayne, any woman can do that."

"No, most fine women only use the half of their brain that keeps them standing, walking, talking, and fucking. Why are you being such a Debbie Downer about my situation now? Your entire conversation was different a month ago.

You're the one that said I need to find one woman that I could see myself having kids and shit with, right?"

"My position hasn't changed. All I'm saying is make sure when you do settle down she has at least 80% of everything you're looking for, including what you already named."

"She does, man, that's what I'm telling you. She is wifey material for me. Don't you think so?

Bryan laughed and said, "Who am I to tell you what you think is right for you? Time will tell, Wayne, I really hope things will work out for you."

"Yeah, I do too, man, because I have a big surprise for her. I put in a bid for this house and she doesn't even know it."

Bryan nodded his head in agreement and left it as simple as that. Who was he to tell Wayne he was making a big mistake. He didn't want to say too much or too little, but he knew deep down inside that something hellish was going to unleash with that woman.

Chapter 2

"This new expense account came right on time huh, Kayla?" mentioned Tasha, condescendingly. Tasha was a nurse from Kayla's new team. Having to deal with a completely new team of catty women was the only bad side of her promotion she had gotten about a year ago. Tasha was tall, dark, skinny and had an amazing bright smile. She put Kayla in the mind of a Naomi Campbell with a terrible attitude problem.

"I guess, but with the money my future husband is making, there really is no need for it," responded Kayla, in a matter-of-fact tone.

Kayla noticed Tasha cutting her eyes at her as Tasha stood in the oversized mirror in Megan's closet. Megan was their boss. The closet was so huge, it was almost the size of a normal master bedroom. Along with Kayla and Tasha were two other co-workers, Chloe and Courtney. They were all invited to Megan's home to plan for her 10th marriage anniversary party.

Chloe and Courtney weren't related, but they acted and looked so much alike that everyone called them work twins. They both were about the same height, size, and had short curly hair.

Kayla didn't really care for them or anyone from the new team, especially Tasha. Most of her team seemed narrow-minded or intimidated by her except for Dexter, who was the only gay male colleague she really hung out with at work. Kayla assumed they were jealous because she was the youngest on the team, owned a new two-story brick home, and was about to marry a handsome and successful man. More importantly, Meg adored Kayla and immediately took her under her wing as if she was her lost daughter. The closer Meg and Kayla got, the more the girls seemed to want to challenge her.

"As much as these men cheat, I wouldn't dare depend on a man's finances to secure me, but I guess that's what separates women from girls," Tasha said and laughed as she high-fived Chloe.

"No, what separates girls from women is when you're woman enough to leave your man after he has a personal all time high record of being unfaithful."

Kayla knew she had gone below the belt, but she was fed up with Tasha always attempting to undercut everything she did or said. Everyone at work knew that every time Tasha's husband was caught cheating, he would send her roses and gifts in attempt to cover up his cheating ways. Dexter always filled Kayla in on the "tea" because he was someone who knew everyone's business at work and outside of work. Why Tasha would continue to try to come for her was ridiculous, but Kayla wasn't having it today. Kayla was one-step away from revealing the rumor about how Tasha's husband was said to be the father of the new nurse assistant's baby.

"Hey ladies, what do you think?" asked Megan, twirling in the closet with a fitted, red-ruffled dress on her size six figure.

Meg had no idea what she just interrupted. For her age, Meg was still gorgeous with full flowing brunette hair, perky breast, and nice peachy skin.

"You are stunning!" replied Tasha, trying to ensure that she beat Kayla to the compliment.

Kayla didn't say a word. She simply watched as Tasha's sidekicks agreed to what she personally thought was one of the most hideous red dresses she had ever seen Meg try to pull off. Although Meg was small, she didn't really have any curves and those ruffles made her look as if she was a skinny chicken with big breast.

"Well, Kayla?" Meg asked, as if Kayla was her dress official.

"Meg, you and I both know you were sexy as hell in that black, off-the-shoulders sequin dress with the deep split. You look smaller than what you already are and you had a little booty showing. Why are we even having this conversation?"

"Kayla, must you be rude everywhere you go?" asked Tasha, cutting her eyes at Meg for approval.

"Pin up some soft curls in your hair and put on those matching sequin stilettos and wear those black diamond earrings your hubby just bought you. Everyone in the room will hate and love you at the same damn time," said Kayla, completely ignoring Tasha's comment.

The room grew silent as Meg twirled in the mirror one last time in her ruffles.

"Meg, I would say go with the red dress, it makes you look vivacious," said Courtney on her Tasha suck-up train.

"No, No…I think Kayla's right on this one. These ruffles make my mid section look flabby, so they probably will make me look at least 10 pounds heavier in my photos. Besides, Dylan has a tailor-made tuxedo and his vest actually matches the sequin in the black dress. What would I do without my Kayla?" asked Meg, smiling and blowing a kiss at Kayla.

"I could think of a few things," responded Tasha.

"Oh, Tasha, you always get so saucy when someone goes against your ideas," Meg said and laughed.

"All I'm saying is the red dress looks fabulous on you."

"Tasha, if you suck up anymore than you already have, then we won't have any more air circulating in this room," mocked Kayla.

"You guys keep me going. I'm going to go get changed, so we can head out to lunch," Meg said, laughing even harder.

"Has being a bitch always gotten you cool points?" challenged Tasha.

Chloe and Courtney looked at Kayla in shock as Kayla rose up from her chair as if she was about to physically respond. She walked closer to Tasha, who was clearly anticipating an altercation in the boss's home.

"Tasha, I think you are a unique person. It really fascinates me to think that you actually think you are just as smart as I am," said Kayla, smiling as she grabbed her purse and exited the closet.

She wasn't going to dare give Tasha any satisfaction that day. She knew when and where to pick her fights. It would only be a matter of time before Tasha tried her at the right place and at the right time.

A few hours later Kayla arrived home to an empty house. Nicholas was spending the night with his cousins at his uncle's home and she knew Bryan had his meeting with his bosses. This gave her the time to do some extra cleaning and unpacking boxes they had thrown in the attic a few months ago when they first moved into their new home. After pouring a glass of wine to help her relax, she went up to the attic, went from box to box, and unpacked pictures, wall decorations, and other items that would be useful to her around the house. She also took down a few large mirrors that Bryan would have to help her hang on the walls once he got home. She headed back up to the attic to finish up for the day and then received a text from Bryan. He told her he was going to have a few drinks with the guys, but when he got home, he had something important he wanted to talk to her about. Kayla agreed, but she was puzzled about what he wanted to discuss. They had just bought the house, so it couldn't be relocating. They definitely weren't having money or sex problems, so what was so important that it had to be singled out as being *important*?

As she was about to turn off the light and head out of the attic, she noticed a half-opened, unfamiliar box that was placed on the far side of the wall towards the back. She knew she didn't put it back there, and she didn't remember seeing it when they moved. It was weird how it was isolated from everything else.

Having to satisfy her curiosity, she brought the box down from the attic, sat it on the couch in their master suite, and opened it. Her heart nearly dropped when she saw several pictures of random women, empty gift boxes, cards, and love letters.

Kayla was furious. Why would Bryan have the audacity to bring his old flings' memories into their new home? They were supposed to get married in less than a month, so what would be the need for him to hold on to this garbage. She continued to look through the box in disgust until she came across the most interesting photo of them all. It was a picture of Wayne's girl, Jesse, in a black two-piece bikini blowing kisses at the photographer, who had to be none other than Bryan. Kayla didn't want her emotions to overcome her rational thinking. Whatever Bryan did years ago before he met her shouldn't interfere with the present. Besides, she really did want to know what it was that Bryan wanted to discuss. She knew if she threw the box in his face, they'd argue all night about it. She decided to wait until the time presented itself to talk about the box. Furthermore, she hid the box in a different spot to see how often, if he did, go back and reminisce on his old baggage.

Chapter 3

Bryan couldn't wait to get home to his fiancée. He told her he was going to get some drinks with the guys, but he actually went to pick up the custom diamond ring he had bought for their wedding. Bryan really wanted to give Kayla the world, especially since he felt he had put her through so much with Jennie Jenson. He was now in an emotional and financial place where he could give her his all. He honestly never thought he would settle down with any woman, less knowing a woman with a son. He actually grew to love Nicholas as his own, and Kayla made him laugh, she respected his wants and needs, she held them both down when Bryan had seasonal work, she sexed him good, she complimented him on a regular, and she kept herself looking good. She was all he hoped for in a woman, so finally he came to a point in his mind and heart where he didn't want to live without her. He took pride in the fact that he was able to provide for them both now, so spending over $7,550 for her wedding ring was just the tip of the iceberg of what he had in store for her.

He walked in the house and saw Kayla relaxed on the living room couch watching television. He went in the kitchen, put his beer in the refrigerator, grabbed two glasses, and brought the wine in the living room where Kayla was sitting.

"Hey my queen, you look amazing," he said, rubbing her soft legs.

"Thanks, what did you want to talk about?" she asked, not noticing how dry and irritated she sounded.

"What's wrong with you?" he asked.

"Nothing, I just had a long day with the girls," she said, trying to hide her true emotions from her experience with his secret box.

"They hatin' on my baby again, huh? Well, I got you something that's really gone make them haters hate."

"Oh really," Kayla said, cutting her eyes back at the television.

Bryan pulled out a small golden box wrapped in a small red ribbon.

"What's this?" Kayla asked.

"Just open it and see, sexy lady."

Kayla slowly opened the box and saw the biggest diamonds she had ever held in her hand.

"Is this for real?" she asked, jumping off the couch and running straight to the mirror to admire the reflection of her hand.

Bryan laughed and said, "I told you I was going to give you everything the world has to offer one day at a time. You are my rock and there is no such thing as life without the one I truly love."

Kayla was too in awe to respond. She was dazed in the mirror with her hand on her upper chest admiring the ring. Bryan walked up behind her and wrapped his arms around her waist.

"Well, do you like it?"

"Do I like it? I'm about to go and put some insurance on this baby."

"You sure know how to keep me smiling," Bryan said.

"I mean, Bryan, this looks like a $10,000 ring!"

"Well, you're close with taxes and all."

"Are you serious? You love me this much?"

"Kayla, yes, I love you this much."

Kayla turned around, pushed Bryan against the wall, and grabbed his face while putting her tongue in his mouth. She ripped off her shirt, then his shirt, and immediately kissed him everywhere on and around his chest. She got down and unzipped his pants, put her hands inside his briefs, and gently began to massage his manhood as she slowly pulled down his briefs. She kissed places around his penis making him yearn for the main action he was about to received. She then stroked the shaft with her tongue and fully indulged it in her mouth as he moaned in gratification.

Feeling himself about to reach his climax, Bryan swiftly got her up and gently tossed her backwards on the couch. He grabbed one side of her booty cheek, tapped and squeezed it, and inserted his hard manhood inside of her. His powerful strokes made her booty clap in rhythm as he tried to hold his climax. Moments later, she began to squeeze a pillow and groan in ecstasy as he felt her body tremble to meet his elation.

After a great session of lovemaking, Bryan figured it would be a good time to discuss with Kayla the details of the plans he and Wayne had made earlier. Wayne got news that he was approved for the home. Bryan talked Wayne into momentarily putting the home in only his name before adding Jesse. However, Wayne needed a small favor and Bryan was praying that Kayla would roll with it. He hoped that she'd still be in awe about those karats he just put on her finger and say yes to just about anything.

"Damn girl, I love you so much, you know that, right?"

"You better, but it slick sounds like you're leading up to something you want to ask or tell me."

"Dang, I can't tell the woman I'm about to marry I love her at any given time?"

"Sure, so what is it you have to tell me?"

Bryan took a deep breath, "Well, listen babe, I just want you to know that Wayne and Alex are trying to plan some type of bachelor party behind my back. I'm not sure what they're trying to do, but they have been asking me to decide on random locations to do landscape, like I'm slow or something."

"Really," she sarcastically responded.

"Damn, baby, why did you have to respond like that, you know I don't get down with ratchet stripper hoes?"

"I know Bryan, but don't bring it to me as if you're going to run out the building when they bring the hoes in or something."

"What building?"

"Anyway Bryan, I don't have time to play with you or your silly friends."

"Speaking of my friends, I have something important I want to talk to you about and before you say no, just here me out completely, okay?"

"I'm listening."

"I had a talk with Wayne and from the moves he has made so far, I know he is in the process of trying to change his life around."

"Oh, he must have gone from nine hoes to eight, okay." She said and laughed.

"Kayla, there you go again judging people. You don't see me making negative comments about them scandalous nurses you work with."

"Hey, I'm just stating the facts and you don't even know the women I work with. I've been around Wayne several times."

"Okay, so when have you personally seen him with someone besides Jesse?"

"I don't have to see him because I hear you on your phone covering for him on a weekly basis."

"Okay, babe, now you're bringing up stuff that happened six months ago."

"Are you serious, Bryan? That was like two weeks ago when I overheard you in the kitchen telling Wayne you got him for the last time."

"Listen babe, I feel that we are rubbing off on him, and he is really turning over a new leaf in his life."

"What is the point in all this, Bryan?"

"Wayne just put a down payment on a new home."

"That's good for him, now he and his hoes can be domesticated," she said and laughed.

"Kayla, can you please stop and be serious for one minute please?" he asked, almost annoyed.

"Wow, you really have been sticking up for him lately, huh?"

"All I'm saying is that you don't know what that man has been through or the facts that led him to act and be the person he is. Anyone can change. Had someone asked me three years ago would I be getting married, I probably would have laughed so hard I would've spit in their face."

"Okay, fair enough. He has changed. Is that it?"

"Well, Dewayne and Jesse's lease is up and they have about a good three weeks before they actually close on their new home, so I told him they could stay here until everything is finalized."

Kayla said, "The conversation was getting a little intense, huh? You always know how to make me laugh babe."

"What is so funny about me keeping my homeboy from being homeless for a few weeks?"

Quickly silenced by the seriousness of his face, Kayla's laugh went from hysterical to distress. She could feel the anxiety overcome her as she failed to control her rage.

"First off, I'm not sure why you would tell someone its okay to cohabitate with you when you don't fuckin' live alone. Secondly, it's beyond me why you would feel comfortable enough to allow another man in your home who may "accidently" walk in on your fiancée naked, and last but not fuckin' least, it will be a cold day in hell before his cunt can lay her head on a pillow in this house."

"Kayla, I love you, but I swear sometimes you have a childish way of handling things."

"Oh, really! Just wait right here and I'll show you a child-like mind."

Kayla went to the closet where she hid Bryan's "fling" box. Once she was back in the room, she dumped all of its contents on top of him.

"What the hell are you doing, girl?"

"Now was my child-like mind supposed to find pictures and notes of you fucking your best friend's fiancée?"

"Man, what is this shit?"

"You know exactly what the hell this is. You took pre-fuck photos of your boy's girl, that's what the hell it is and several other photos of random bitches you took down through there."

"First off, you need to calm down because I didn't even know that box was here. That had to have been something my mom grabbed when she was helping us move. Furthermore, what the fuck are you doing going through my shit?"

"Our shit…and if you thought for one minute that I would accept a ridiculous proposal of that whore being here, then you clearly played them and yourself."

"Why are you flipping out over something that happened damn near 10 years ago? All this shit is old."

"From the way that bitch made sure I knew that she use to fuck you, lets me know exactly where her head is."

"Babe, she said that she knew me back from the college days, nothing like what you're making it out to be."

Kayla continued as if Bryan hadn't said a word. "Now, in the event that her family will not allow him to stay with them, then I get it, he can chill here on two conditions. One, as long as you are here when he is here and the muthafucka better not have a key or try to leave a window open so he can sneak his cunt in when we're not here."

"Baby, listen. There is nothing about that girl that I could possibly want. I'm just trying to help a friend. Can you please understand that?

"Okay, well, while we're passing out rooms, how about I invite Nicholas's dad to chill too, and we can all be one got damn happy family."

"Kayla, calm the fuck down. I get it. I'll talk to him and see if we can figure something else out."

"You know what, for you to even suggest that hoe come stay here got me feeling some type of way."

"Oh my gosh, Kayla, what the fuck? I just put a car on your damn hand and this is the thanks I get!"

"I bet Wayne doesn't even know you smashed her, does he?

"Ashes to ashes and dust to dust, Kayla, that shit is dead."

"And so is this night. You have a good time resting by yourself."

Kayla grabbed her pillow and stormed out of the room as she slammed the door behind her.

Chapter 4

The next morning Kayla woke up to scrambled eggs, bacon, sausage, a banana muffin, and strawberries with a large glass of apple juice beside her plate. Bryan also left a note that stated he was sorry for not considering her feelings and added a huge 'I LOVE YOU' at the end. Even though Kayla was impressed with his attempt to get back in her good graces, she was still not at ease by the fact that Bryan had already agreed to allow someone he had sex with to come stay with them. Although he didn't know until during the argument that she had found his private box, he knew from the time at Wayne's barbeque that she was suspicious about him and Jesse. As she sat down and ate, Kayla's mind went several different places the more she thought about Bryan's suggestion. She wondered had he and Jesse already been secretly seeing one another behind her back or if Bryan was trying to find a slick way to get his rocks off one last time before he got married. She just couldn't figure out why her fiancé would feel comfortable presenting such a ridiculous idea to her.

Not wanting to continue to entertain her idle mind with distracting thoughts, she decided to go to the hospital a little early to see if she could catch up with Dr. Roberts. It had been a while since she had to request anxiety medication from him, but things seemed to be getting out of hand once again. She didn't intend on making it a habit, but she could feel her anxiety becoming more frequent as layers of problems began to pile from every angle. She decided to get her things situated first before she made the stop to his office.

As she walked through the long white halls on her way to her station, something seemed eerie in the air. Perhaps the temperature seemed a bit colder than normal or maybe it was all in her mind. She tried to shake the feeling off and just as she rounded the corner, she saw the last familiar face she wanted to see.

"Officer Perez?" she questioned as her heart began to flutter.

"Kayla, hello, it's good seeing you again," he said and smiled.

Although Kayla had a feeling he was coming to bear bad news, she couldn't ignore the fact that Officer Perez was even sexier than she remembered.

"Well…I would say it's nice to see you as well, but uhm…I'm not really sure what I should say," she responded, looking over at his new female partner.

"We really need you to come down to the station. There is a high priority matter that we have to confidentially speak to you about," he stated, shifting into a more serious tone.

Kayla was very apprehensive, but Officer Perez never gave her any problems.

She was happy not to see his former bald partner, but she definitely didn't trust the new Betty he was with, so she decided not to make conversation until she was alone with Officer Perez. She wasn't comfortable sitting in the back seat of the squad car, but it wasn't as if she was in handcuffs, so she dealt with it. She tried to eavesdrop on the conversation they were having up front in hopes of trying to figure out why they wanted to question her. Unfortunately, she only picked up bits and pieces of what she thought she heard about manslaughter.

Once they arrived at the precinct, Kayla was escorted into what seemed like the exact same room she was in a few years ago when they interrogated her about Bryan. She watched Perez and his partner thoroughly looking through some type of folder from the glass window in the room. About twenty minutes later, she noticed Officer Perez passing the folder to, low and behold, his former partner, balding Officer Kelly. He walked in the room with the folder and threw it on the table.

"You are going to tell me everything you know about these four people," he demanded, spreading out the photos on the table. It was a picture of Dana Foster, her deceased ex roommate. The other photos were Dana's cousin Jessica and her husband, George, along with a photo of Dana's mother, Ms. Catherine.

Kayla began to tear up as she saw Dana's photo. It instantly brought back the last memories she had of Dana telling her that George was going to kill her. If only she had believed in Dana's accusations at the time, maybe she could have helped her. A tear rolled down her cheek as she began to speak.

"I think we both are aware that this was my roommate who died about five or six years ago and-"

"Wait, you mean your roommate who was murdered about five or six years ago, right?" Officer Kelly rudely interrupted, totally ignoring Kayla's sensitivity.

"The last I heard, yes, Officer Friendly, she was murdered," she said, sneering back.

"Look, Ms. McQueen, I'm not here to be your friend. I'm here to solve a case. Now, did you ever see or meet these two individuals?" he asked, pointing at Jessica and George's photo.

"Yes, I did."

"Okay, so who are they?"

"Her name is Jessica and his name is George." Kayla was being evasive and wasn't willing to offer any additional information to this jerk cop.

"That doesn't answer who they are."

"It does to me."

"You're trying to be difficult, ma'am, and you're making it harder for yourself. Who are these people in reference to Dana Foster?"

"Jessica is Dana's cousin, and George is Jessica's husband."

"Are you good friends with all of these people?"

"No, I'm not. Like you just said, Dana was murdered, so she's my former good friend."

"Okay you little smart ass, you just said that you know these people, so there had to have been some type of interaction at some point in order for you to be introduced to them," he replied.

"We all went to a party once and that's about it."

"And that's the only time you saw these individuals?"

"Pretty much."

"Okay, so explain to me how we have video footage of you, Jessica, and Catherine Foster at your work place about a year ago."

"Well, clearly I can't prevent people from coming to a public hospital."

"You know something, people like you disgust me. I don't think you realize how serious this is, Miss! This is a double and could possibly be a triple murder case and we don't have time for smart asses like you!"

Kayla was having fun pissing him off until he pulled out a photo from the folder of a little handsome boy who had Dana's eyes. This was the first time she had seen a photo of him.

"Wait…what do you mean a double murder case?"

"Oh, now you want to get serious, huh?"

"Is this who I think it is?"

"This is the missing grandson of this woman who was found murdered in an abandoned warehouse two days ago by some damn kids!" he screamed.

"No!" she protested.

"Yes, and would you like to know how they found her? Her throat was cut from one end to the other, almost severing her head."

"Ms. Catherine!" Kayla said as she sobbed.

"Look Miss, I know this is a lot to take in, but you must tell us everything you know about these people and any additional information that you can remember Dana giving you."

Kayla was so sad that she couldn't do anything, but cry. She was only trying to protect her son and herself, but she didn't know that someone would be ruthless enough to kill an elderly woman. She thought it would have died down, and everyone would go their separate ways. She assumed Ms. Catherine must have found out the truth, so they had to get rid of her. Kayla couldn't hold back anymore. She knew that a kid's life was at stake and maybe even hers.

"Ms. Catherine came up to my job and told me she was launching her own private investigation about the murder of her daughter. She was asking me questions about a 'Mr. Goodbar' who is unknown to me. Then Dana-" she stopped.

"Go ahead, Kayla, what did Dana say?" Officer Kelly eagerly asked.

Kayla was scared. She didn't want to say anything. If she told them what she knew, they might accuse her of withholding information. They would also insinuate that her information could have save the life of Ms. Catherine. She had to think of something basic.

"She said that she was super excited about her baby, but in fear of their lives because someone was leaving her threatening messages," Kayla finally responded.

"Who was leaving her threatening messages?"

"I don't know," Kayla said as she began to cry.

"Think got damn it!" he yelled.

"I don't know you selfish asshole, my friend was murdered!"

"Calm down, Miss."

Kayla was literally getting sick of him and this entire investigation. No one seemed to get her or have any concern about her or her son's safety. It seemed as if they didn't want to be under the heat for allowing the case to manifest. She decided to turn up the heat toward him.

"If Ms. Catherine is dead, then where is the kid?"

Totally thrown off by the question, Officer Kelly circled the room with his hands resting on what little hair he had left on his head.

"Ms. McQueen that is what we are trying to find out. We need to find that boy before anything else happens. Do you remember anything at all that could lead us to the boy's whereabouts?" he politely asked.

At that moment, Kayla realized it was something about finding that boy that made this personal for Officer Kelly. She wondered was this the last time he had to drop the ball on the department. Although she disliked him, she thought about what it would be like to lose Nicholas. She couldn't even bare the thought.

"Jessica said that I didn't have to worry about ever hearing from Ms. Catherine again. She said that she had everything covered."

As soon as she made her statement, another officer walked in the room, put a pen down along with a pad, and asked for her statement in writing. Just as Kayla was about to pick up the pen, the door opened once again.

"Kayla McQueen, you put that pen down this instance and come with me," demanded a sexy, green-eyed man in a black tailored suit, "Officer Kelly, this is my client, Kayla McQueen."

"Get this rich boy out of my face," responded Officer Kelly, storming out of the room.

"I would suggest you guys contact me if you have any questions regarding my client. We wouldn't want another misunderstanding now would we. Shall we?" he said, motioning to Kayla as he escorted her out of the door.

Kayla was confused about what just happened and how this stranger even knew her name let alone the situation going on. Once outside, the attorney walked her over to his black Lexus Rx 350.

"I definitely need to know who you are and what is going on before I get in this car with a complete stranger."

"I am the man who just saved your life and I'm sure by looking at me and the car we're about to get into, you already know there's no reason for foul play. Get in," he said, opening her door and quickly going around to the driver's side before she even stepped foot in.

"Get in," he repeated in almost a yelling tone.

Kayla got in with this strange man, not knowing who he was or where he was about to take her.

Chapter 5

Kayla stared out her window as he slowly moved the car from its parked position. She wasn't sure whether to jump out or wait until he offered information. The only thing that was keeping her seated was the fact that everything about this man was sexy. The way he talked, the way he walked, and even his ego at the precinct and getting her into the car was a turn on. The Lexus was fully loaded, super clean, and smelled nice. She thought about the fact that he happened to know her full name and he knew where to find her. No one could have just predicted she would be down at the police station. It gave her some comfort that he obviously was sent by someone she knew, but who?

"My name is Jared Mancini and I work for your boss, Meg. I am Meg's personal attorney," he began as if he was reading her thoughts.

"Meg sent you?"

"Yes, I know this is weird getting into the car with someone you've never met, but I want you to trust me."

"Trust would definitely go both ways in a situation like this."

"I agree. Well, perhaps I should tell you a little about myself. I have been Meg's personal attorney for the last five years, but I've known her since I was a kid. I started working for my dad's law office as soon as I graduated and now I'm here. I haven't lost a case yet and I don't plan on losing one."

"I guess that's all I need to know for now."

"I definitely would like to build a trusting business relationship with you as long as you feel that's something you're willing to do."

"We can work on it," she responded.

"That works for me. First things first, tell me all I need to know about this case. I need to know if they have anything on you or if there is something out there that could possibly get you locked up."

"Well, my roommate was killed about five or six years ago and there has been an ongoing investigation that went cold."

"Okay, so that leads me to assume your roommate gave you information that the cops feel you're withholding, so since the case as been elevated, they have decided to harass you."

"That sums it up. How do you know all of this?"

"Kayla, we're building trust here, remember? I am a very resourceful person, and you'll see that in the days to come."

Kayla sat back and thought about the situation at hand. She hadn't had anyone to confide in about the Dana Foster case. Although she gave Bryan minor details, she never told even him the full story.

She wasn't really sure if she should tell this guy either. For all she knew he could have a tape recorder and be playing the field for the other side. She was very perplexed, but she was also tired of holding this huge ordeal in for so long. She also wanted Dana's son to have a chance if he was still alive. She still couldn't understand how the baby survived if Dana was murdered. Did someone find her just in time to save the baby, or was her killer bold enough to take her to a hospital? It seemed so strange because Kayla knew an unborn baby had limited time after the mother stopped breathing or if she lost a certain amount of blood. *Why weren't the police investigating that aspect of it?* she wondered.

"Is there something extra I need to know?" he asked, interrupting Kayla's thoughts.

"I didn't tell the officers that Dana told me she was having an affair with her cousin's husband. She said when she told him the baby was his baby, he said he didn't want it."

"Kayla, I'm going to be honest with you, that's a lot to withhold. That is motive and intent on behalf of her cousin's husband. Did you ever personally speak to this man?"

"Not really. He called my phone around the time of her pregnancy and made an indication I should keep quiet about anything I possibly knew if I knew what was good for me."

"Kayla, are you aware of how serious this is?"

"I wanted it just to go away and it did, for a while, until Ms. Catherine was killed and her grandson went missing."

"It baffles me that something simple, like you trying to do the right thing by going to college and bettering yourself, ends up with you being involved in a double-murder-missing-child case."

"How did you know I went to college?" Kayla asked, now very suspicious of who he really was and his intent.

"Kayla, I read all the files before I decided to take the case. Meg and I may be cool, but I'm not an "any case taking" type of guy."

"Oh, well, that's all I know," she said.

"I know this ordeal is probably spinning you in circles, but I really need to know everything you know about this case."

"That's everything I have, sir."

"Sir? No, please call me, Jay. Anyone who is a personal friend of Meg is definitely likely to become a personal friend of mine."

"Thanks, I wish I could tell you more, but that's all I have. Dana didn't tell me everything; she just told me what she wanted me to know. To be honest, she had a few guy friends, so any one of them could have easily gotten jealous of her being pregnant."

"Yeah, but they wouldn't have wacked granny."

"Yeah, I guess," she softly replied.

"I'm sorry if that was too insensitive. I definitely have to work on that. Continue if you will."

"In the beginning I thought she was just jealous of her cousin's beauty and the wealthy lifestyle her cousin lived. However, when the cop came to our apartment and told me she was dead, I knew it was more to it. I tried to pretend as if it was a bad dream that would go away. I never would have thought her grandmother would become a victim.

For some reason a part of me wants to believe this is a joke or someone trying to make a movie. This is the type of stuff I watch on television. How am I connected to an animal that would kill an elderly lady?"

"You sure have a way of coping with things and I wish I could give you the answers."

"I know things like this exist, I'm not naïve. There wouldn't be such thing as a grand jury or death penalty if they didn't. I'm just saying why would it have to be my life?"

"Unfortunately, this shit is real, but the good news is, if you're telling all that you know, then you're nothing more than a key witness," he said, reassuring her.

"No, I would never jeopardize my son's life by going on the stand. I would plead the fifth to everything I know."

Jared laughed and said, "Wow, you do watch a lot of television. The prosecution would make a mockery out of you if you did that."

"You can't make a mockery out of someone you won't be able to find."

"Whoa, I see that you're serious. I apologize. I should definitely try to put myself in your shoes. I honestly didn't know you had a son. That wasn't ever mentioned."

"Well, I do and he comes first."

A few minutes later, they pulled up at the hospital parking lot. Jared hadn't said a word to her since she had threatened to flee. Maybe he didn't take her seriously until she made that statement. It seemed as if his intent towards her changed or maybe she was reading too much into it.

"Kayla, I want you to put my number in your phone. I am now your personal attorney, so I don't want you to go anywhere or make any statements without you telling me first, okay?"

"Sure," she responded.

"I am serious. I will be in touch with you very soon," he said, giving her his card before driving off.

Kayla was exhausted, but she knew she had to speak with Meg. Now more than ever, she also needed to get with Dr. Roberts as soon as she could. As she knocked on Meg's office door, she felt herself being overwhelmed, frightened, and exhausted at the same time.

"Kayla, are you okay?" Meg asked, rushing up to hug Kayla.

"I feel like I'm about to lose it," Kayla said and sobbed, with tears rolling down her face.

"Oh Honey, it's okay. How serious is it?"

"It's a murder case, Meg. My roommate was killed years back and now her mother was killed and the surviving son of my roommate is missing."

"Oh goodness, Kayla, are you serious?"

"Yes, I am. I was living in Atlanta and going to college. I had no idea that I had surrounded myself with real life criminals at the top of the most wanted list."

"Kayla, I am so sorry that you are going through all of this. I had no idea that a young, sweet, and beautiful person like you would be dealing with such a huge ordeal."

"I still honestly can't believe it myself."

"Well, honey, don't worry. As soon as I heard those two cops came and dragged you down the hall, I immediately called my personal attorney, who has a hundred percent success rate."

"Yeah, Jared seems great. Thank you so much for your help."

"Kayla, we're family. You don't have to thank me for this. I also have two condos in Nashville and one condo in Knoxville if you ever need to take time off and get away."

"Thank you, Meg; I can't begin to tell you how much I appreciate you. No one has looked out for me like this outside of my mom, and I am forever indebted to you."

"Kayla, I've always told you that you're like a daughter to me. If it's in my hands, I will get it done, okay?"

"Thank you so much," cried Kayla, embracing Meg with another hug.

"I've got to get this paperwork done and then I have a meeting with Gabby."

"Gabby?"

"Well, the board wants to discuss giving her a second chance to redeem herself. She explained how she was threatened and beaten by her ex-boyfriend, who is now in jail and who ultimately led her to make all the terrible decisions she made."

"So where would she work?" asked Kayla, tensing up. She had instantly forgotten about the entire Dana ordeal.

"If they allow her to come back, she will follow you until she's able to resume her lead position, but don't worry, you two would head the department together."

"Meg, you know this girl is bad news. I told you about how she gave my ex boyfriend Raymond, confidential information about me that could have gotten my son and I killed. How could they reconsider someone like her?"

"Kayla, I am on your side, but you know her dad is a pillar of the community and has a lot of pull in this town. If it was up to me, personally the little whore would be somewhere on the streets. Unfortunately, this wasn't my call."

Kayla had to think fast. She knew that she and Gabby couldn't be in the same place ever again in peace. For all she knew, Raymond could have been sending orders from jail for her to finish the job he started. She had to think of something to persuade Meg in her favor. She knew just the thing to get Meg riled up.

"Meg, this cannot happen. I do not trust her and she is a demon. She even told me how she hated Dr. Roberts and she would find a way to expose his extra curricular activities."

"Wait, what?" Meg asked, now curious.

"Well, Gabby and I were actually friends before things started going south. I was still fairly new to the floor, but I remember her telling me how Dr. Roberts had side jobs going on with his nurses that were illegal. She said her dad would soon own Dr. Roberts."

"Kayla, are you sure?"

"Well, I've never personally seen Dr. Roberts do anything wrong and once Gabby left the hospital, I no longer was concerned."

"This is interesting. I have to go run a quick errand. Thank you, Kayla, I'll see you at the anniversary party," Meg said, almost tripping over her own floor plant.

Kayla hated lying, but she had to. She remembered Meg exposing her breast in the swimming pool at one of Dr. Roberts's old parties, so there was no telling what Meg did after Kayla left. In fact, Meg would have also had to know about Dr. Roberts spiking the wine with prescription pills, since Kayla found out that Meg was actually the host of all Dr. Roberts's parties. The newer socialites to those parties were probably unaware of why they were feeling so frisky. She knew that Meg wouldn't want information like that to get out around the hospital, so Kayla embellished what she told her. Now that Kayla had her lead position, she was willing to do anything to keep it.

Chapter 6

Arriving home after work, Kayla was drained. She ran into Dr. Roberts before leaving the hospital, and he provided her with a script of anxiety medicine. He also said he had something important to discuss with her, so they set up a private meeting for the following day. Kayla hoped whatever the meeting was about wouldn't overwhelm her more than she already felt.

After taking a few pills, all she wanted to do was take a long shower and lie down in her king-sized bed. She pulled up in her driveway and noticed an unfamiliar car blocking the entrance to her garage. Immediately, her relaxed mood shifted to rage as she went in to confront the guilty party of the unknown car. She walked into the living room and saw Nicolas sitting on the floor playing cards with Jesse. Kayla felt exhausted from being through so much in the course of eight hours. Although she planned to see her fiancé and kid, Jesse was the last face she wanted to see. Jesse's face was a representation of all women that were like scrap dogs searching for anything they could get their paws on and lick dry. She knew that she was about to explode with rage, and there wasn't anything anyone could say or do to calm her down.

"Whose car is blocking my got damn garage?"

"I'm sorry Kay-Kay, I wasn't even thinking. I was so excited about my boo getting a new car that I forgot I blocked the garage," responded Wayne, getting up to go move it.

Bryan looked at Kayla as if she was a total stranger. He couldn't believe she would come in and make a scene like she did. He was beginning to believe that Kayla was jealous of Jesse.

"Kayla, let me talk to you for a minute in private," he demanded, pulling her hand and walking in the kitchen.

"Bryan, I am really not in the mood for any bullshit right now."

"Are you serious? You came home on some bullshit, Kayla, in front of the baby. What is your damn problem?"

"He is six and obviously he's heard worse or did you forget the fact that he got stuffed in a closet by your ex whore's son?"

"Kayla, the fact that you are bringing that up is absurd when you know we're trying to build a solid foundation for our future. What is wrong with you? Are you having nightmares? Do you need a counselor?"

"Excuse me you guys, just came in to grab a few beers," interrupted Jesse, rudely continuing to walk toward the refrigerator.

Bryan could feel Kayla tense up and knew he had to intervene before matters got worse.

"Uhm…Jesse, as you can already see, I'm trying to have a private conversation with my wife."

"I'm sorry; I didn't mean to interrupt you and your fiancée. Wayne asked me would I grab some beers while he promptly moved the car as Kayla requested," she said, walking out the kitchen.

"If that bitch is not out of my house in the next 60 seconds, I'm going to be right back at the police station, this time, in shackles."

"When the hell did you go to the police station? Kayla, what are you talking about?"

Kayla suddenly felt a string of emotions overcoming her as she moved away from Bryan. She took a deep breath, sat down on the chair stool, and began to cry. Bryan followed her as he grabbed her hands and sat beside her.

"Talk to me, baby, what's wrong?"

"I think the people who killed Dana and Ms. Catherine are going to hunt me down and kill me, too," she said as tears began to roll down her cheeks.

"Who are Ms. Catherine and Dana? Are you talking about your old roommate?"

"Yes…two officers came to my job today and took me down to the police station. They sat me down in an interrogation room and told me someone basically decapitated Ms. Catherine's head and her grandson is missing. Catherine is Dana's mom."

"Baby, are you taking any medicines that I may need to know about," Bryan paused as he squinted at her, "or is there something you've been exposed to at the hospital? I have to admit that this sounds crazy."

"I'm serious got damn it and for you to insinuate that I'm delusional is a fucking insult to my intelligence!"

"Baby, calm down. You have to look at this from my perspective. My phone has been on all day and never once did you call or text me about this whole ordeal. I can't even remember the last time you brought this up."

"I didn't because I tried to brush it off. I thought maybe it was over until the officers told me about Ms. Catherine being killed."

"So this is all for real?"

"No, Bryan, I like playing make-believe with you. What the hell do you think?"

"Okay, baby, I'm going to run you a hot bath, so you can relax and get some rest. Don't worry about them, I will send them home and then come back, give you a massage, and we can talk about this some more."

Bryan took Kayla through the back stairs in order to avoid Jesse and Wayne. He was worried that Kayla wasn't getting enough sleep, had too much on her plate with the wedding, and then her boss was asking her to do something every five minutes. He remembered Kayla telling him about the roommate that died years back, but what she was saying now sounded bizarre.

After helping Kayla settle in the tub, Bryan went back downstairs to tell his guests that he and Kayla were calling it a night. Once he got down to the living room, he saw Jesse sitting on the sofa with her legs folded and shoes off. Before he jumped to conclusions, he went into the kitchen and looked out the window to see if their car was still outside.

"Where the hell is Wayne?" he asked, trying not to sound irritated as he walked back into the living room.

"He said that he wanted to give you and me some time alone," Jesse answered, with a mischievous smile.

"Look, call Wayne and tell him to come back right now because we're calling it a night."

"Bryan, do you ever feel like we have unfinished business?" she asked, slowly walking toward him.

"Jesse, you and I both know anything that we had to discuss was years ago and now, I would really appreciate it if you excused yourself from our home."

"Ha, ha, ha…that was cute, Bryan, I mean really? Are you seriously acting as if you don't think about fucking me when you see this ass? I know deep down inside you wish it was me lying in your bed naked every night," she said, lifting up her shirt and exposing her double D bra.

A younger Bryan would have bent her over, busted one, and then sent her ass on her way, but not now. Not only was his best friend serious about this broad, but his fiancée was upstairs and could walk down any second. Her actions actually disgusted and infuriated him all in one.

"Jesse, I am a pretty decent guy, but if you even think for one minute that I will allow you to disrespect my fiancée while you're in our home, I will literally throw your ass outside and you will wait out there until someone comes to get you. I'm sure your sister is thanking you right now for holding down her legacy."

When Bryan saw the look on Jesse's face, he knew he took it too far, but he didn't know what else to do. This girl was relentless and had no regard for anything, so she needed a dose of reality.

"Wow," she said, putting her shirt back on, grabbing her purse, and opening the door. "You know something, Bryan; I don't know why you're pretending to be this good wholesome guy all of a sudden. When it's all said and done, you still had sex with me behind your best friend's back. Then to make matters worse, you're marrying a girl that was the girlfriend of the son of the married woman you were screwing. See you in hell, Bro."

He slammed and locked the door behind her. He knew that his words punished her more than a slap on her jaw. Back in college, Jesse had told Bryan that her sister was a well-known escort, who used a portion of her money to help pay for Jesse's tuition. Jesse had begged her sister to quit, and promised her sister that she would get a part-time job. Her sister, Justice, was making over $3,000 a week and refused to quit. Halfway into Jesse's junior year of college, Justice was found raped and beaten in her upscale apartment. By the time Jesse got to the hospital, her sister had lost too much blood and died shortly after. To make matters worse, the doctors confirmed she was nine weeks pregnant. Jesse didn't know about the pregnancy before the murder, but she assumed her sister did, since there were parenting magazines found when they went to clean out her apartment.

Bryan felt bad, but not bad enough to chase her down the street. He was more upset by the fact that she made a move on him while his future wife was only a few steps away. It was disrespectful to him and Kayla. How could he have explained something like that to Kayla had she walked down the stairs and saw Jesse with her shirt off and him standing there in front of her?

Kayla had already found a dumb ass box of letters and photos, which he had no idea why his mom would bring to their home, so he knew all hell would have broke loose had Kayla saw them. He was that much more thankful that Kayla went to bed early.

Bryan went into the kitchen to pour himself a few shots of Hennessy before going back up to Kayla, since he still had a lot on his mind. Jesse's reference to Ms. Jenson only made him think of the death of Mr. Jenson and how he would still be alive if it wasn't for the affair with Jennie. He wondered if God would forgive him for his mistake, or would karma somehow come back to him by Kayla being unfaithful. He took a few more shots before going up to the bedroom.

"What took you so long, daddy?" asked Kayla, straddling a pillow in a black laced teddy and matching stilettos.

Bryan was completely shocked and unprepared for what he saw. If anything, he imagined Kayla under the covers in a fetal-like position from the way she was acting thirty minutes ago.

"I'm hoping you're speechless in a good way," she continued, positioning herself on the edge of the bed, seductively opening and closing her legs.

"Uhm...babe, are you feeling okay?

"Well, I'd be feeling a lot better if I had you inside me."

Bryan didn't understand what all just took place in the course of an hour, but Kayla sitting there in her fishnets gave him a hard-on that was almost too painful.

While his mind was still on the fact that he had to deal with Wayne about Jesse, his body was ready to thrust up into Kayla.

"Wait," she said, locking the door, "I got something I want you to put on me."

She grabbed some warming KY lubricant out of the closet and handed it to Bryan. He pulled the panty portion of the laced teddy to the side and gently began massaging her clitoris.

The warming sensation from the lubricant sent Kayla into a moaning frenzy. She began to ball the covers into her fist from the sensual pleasure, which aroused Bryan twice more than what he was already feeling. He gently flipped her over and somehow managed to keep her lace panties to the side. He positioned her body in a crawl-like position as she met his embrace by placing both elbows on the bed. He swiftly slid inside her like a sleigh on a sheet of ice. He pulled her hips toward him to impact the insertion of his penis. The flapping of her buttocks underneath her fishnets made him go deeper and faster as she began to instruct him to do so. Bryan could feel all the tension inside him about to release as he fell on top of her back and passionately gripped her hair in both hands. Another prompt, slow push made him empty all of his manhood contents inside her shaking body. It was undeniably one of the best sexual explodes he'd ever remembered having. As he kissed her on the top of her head, he knew from thereon that he only had two options. He would die with this woman or either for this woman.

Chapter 7

Kayla woke up the next morning dazed and confused about the night before. She wasn't sure how and why she felt extremely milky between her legs or why she was wearing what she was wearing. She looked over towards Bryan, who had already left, and saw a note on the end table. The note told her how fascinating she was last night and how he couldn't wait to spend the rest of his life with her. The bottom of the note instructed her to go shopping with the $500 he left beneath it. Kayla felt overwhelmed because she didn't even remember what prompted his fascination. Her last memories of yesterday's events were her seeing Nicolas on the floor with Jesse. She sat down on her Victorian chair in order to collect her thoughts. She remembered going to the police station up until arriving home. She hadn't drank anything, so she was puzzled about why she couldn't remember last night's events. She reached for her purse that was on the table beside the bed to get out her cell phone. Lying beside the phone was the bottle of anxiety pills that Dr. Roberts gave her at the hospital. She opened the bottle, took one out, and the inscription on the pill was something she'd never seen. She wondered, *Did Dr. Roberts drug me?*

After she did some morning cleaning and put on her scrubs, Kayla wanted to get to Dr. Roberts office as soon as possible. She had to know what type of medicine he had given her. She wasn't sure how she would approach him because whatever it was, she sort of liked it. She remembered feeling calm and relaxed for a while until she could barely remember anything at all. The more she thought about it, her memory of last nights' events was starting to come back. She remembered being some type of sex maniac and wanting Bryan to pound her body like a wrestler. Now that she could recall what happened, she actually wanted more pills.

Kayla grabbed the keys from her purse and headed out the door. She decided to talk to Dr. Roberts about the side effects to the medicine, as opposed to telling him what really happened, but then again, maybe he already knew what would happen. Just as she was getting into her car, her phone rang.

"Hey, Sweetie, how are you this morning?" asked Meg.

"Hi, Meg, I'm fine. I'm actually headed up to the hospital right now."

"Well, listen, I got a call from Jared today and he wants you to stop by his office. He said that he forgot to get your number and he had something important to tell you about your case."

"Oh, okay. Did he say whether or not it would take long?"

"No Dear, but don't worry about your rounds today, I have you covered."

"Thanks Meg, you're the best. I still plan to come there after the meeting. I have some things I need to discuss with Dr. Roberts."

"Oh, okay. Well, I'll see you later, take care."

After Meg sent her a text with Jared's office address, she put it into her GPS, so she wouldn't have a problem finding it. She looked down at her scrubs and figured she may need to change. She quickly ran into the house and put on her black knee-length pencil skirt, a white blouse, and a black blazer. She accented the outfit with a white pearl necklace and a pair of black heels. She grabbed the curlers, put a few loose curls in her hair, and let it flow. Instead of looking like a client, Kayla looked as if she was about to join his law firm.

About 25 minutes later, Kayla pulled up to a large brick building that had an engraved signed that read MANCINI AND SONS in stone. At that moment, Kayla realized that Jared could not only talk the talk, but he was actually walking the walk. She walked into the revolving doors feeling a tad bit overwhelmed, but you couldn't tell from her appearance. She walked to the massive desk in the corridor and asked the secretary for Jared Mancini.

"And who are you?" unpleasantly asked the receptionist.

"Hello, Kayla. I'm down this way," yelled Jared from the end of the hall.

"He knows who I am," replied Kayla, smirking while walking off and giving an extra twitch in her hips. She could tell that the receptionist was burning her back with an evil stare, but she didn't care. The bitch was rude and shouldn't greet clients that way.

Kayla walked in Jared's office and took notice of the many achievements he had on the walls and his desk. Although she respected him for taking pride in his work, it was a bit too much. It appeared to her that he wanted people to feel impressed or maybe even intimidated by his success, but this was a turn off to Kayla.

She didn't admire men who overindulged in themselves. To her, it meant that he would be too concerned about himself to consider a woman's thoughts and opinions. All these assumptions regarding Jared led her to one huge question. He clearly didn't need the money and he probably figured she couldn't afford him even if he did, so what made him want to take her case, and what was Meg getting out the deal?

"Wow, forgive me if this is unprofessional, but you look quite ravishing," he said, breaking into her thoughts.

"Thank you," she responded without a smile.

"Confident I see. I like it. Please, have a seat. So…Meg said you wanted to see me about your case." He added, leaning on his desk in front of Kayla.

"Did she? Well, I guess we're both under the wrong impression because I was told you had some information for me."

"Uhm…well, yes, I do actually."

"Look, Jared. Contrary to what you may think about me, I am a very intuitive and observant young woman. Just because I'm African American doesn't mean I need a hand out. I also know that you don't need the money or the recognition for this case, so what is the real deal on you being my attorney?

"Are you saying that you don't want me to work your case for you?"

"I am saying that I don't need you to stray from the question."

"I don't know about you, but I am starving. Do you mind if we talk about this over lunch, on me, of course?" he offered.

"Only if I can get the truth."

"I would like to discuss the matter in a different setting where the walls won't echo."

Kayla got up as Jared escorted her out into the hallway. They made a detour out of a back entrance of the building. He led her to his Lexus and drove from the parking lot.

"I have been practicing law for a long time with many successes, Ms. McQueen. I can assure that all of this will go away as if it never happened. The reason why I am telling you this is because the "why" of why I took the case doesn't matter. A young boy is missing and the mother of your deceased roommate was found with her head practically chopped off. You were once involved with all parties. In all reality, you need a lawyer. The circumstances that come behind of why I am taking this case pro bono for you will not directly affect you."

"Okay, so there is a deeper reason and you just can't tell me. Well, I'm smart enough to know that nothing in this life comes free, so somewhere somehow, someone is going to feel like I owe them."

Jared pulled up to an upscale restaurant not far from his office. He got out and opened the door for Kayla. They walked up to the hostess stand, and without a word, a young lady standing there immediately seated Jared at a window table with Victorian chairs.

"I guess this would be very impressive to a woman you were trying to date, huh?"

Jared gave Kayla a mysterious look, but didn't say anything. He ordered drinks for them in his Italian language and must have said something intriguing since the waiter looked at her and winked.

"Meg hasn't told me much about you. It would be helpful if I knew more about my client."

"Well, what has she told you so far and I will fill in the rest of what you need to know."

"Fair enough. She told me you were one of the hardest working nurses she has and you were gorgeous, which I can see for myself. She also told me you have a son."

"Yes, Nicholas. He is the pride and joy of my life. I don't get to see him a lot because of all the crazy hospital hours, but there's nothing I wouldn't do for him."

"Is the child's father in the picture?"

"No, but I have an awesome fiancé who adores him dearly."

"Oh, I guess Meg left off the details of you getting married soon."

"Well, she initially didn't tell you about my son either, so I guess she assumed details didn't matter. I mean, why would it?"

"Oh... it doesn't. I just...didn't know."

"Yeah, but you say that as if it's a disappointment."

"Well, honestly, you are beautiful," he said, staring fiercely in her eyes.

Kayla didn't know how to take what he was saying. He had complimented her several times already, and he seemed taken-back by her engagement. She wondered, *is Meg trying to hook me up, knowing I'm getting married?*

"I have to ask, did you take the case because you thought I was single?"

"No, Kayla. I honestly took the case because I really do owe Meg a huge favor. I just didn't know I was taking the case for someone like you."

"Like me? You barely even know me."

"You can tell a lot about a person within the first few minutes of conversation. I've already learned that you're determined, ambitious, smart, loyal, and I don't have to tell you again how stunning you are."

"Okay, so does this mean you don't want the case anymore since I'm about to get married?"

"No, it just means I'll work harder to pay back my deed with Meg and make sure you are safe at home with your son."

"Well, I really do appreciate it and I hope everything turns out in everyone's favor."

"I can definitely say that Meg is a one of a kind lady and makes things work in her favor."

"Is she a friend of your mom or dad?"

"Meg and my dad went to law school together and became good friends. When my mom and dad divorced, Meg financially helped my dad after my mom sucked him dry and left my dad with nothing but my sister and me."

"Oh, well, looking at that huge building with your name on it, I'm sure your dad has made even with Meg."

"Your lunch madam," interrupted the waiter.

"Let's eat," Jared said, ignoring her comment.

Kayla knew it would be inappropriate to ask about the debt with Meg. There had to be more to it than what he was telling her.

Jared made small talk about past cases and clients as they ate. Kayla noticed him scouring the restaurant as if he was looking or waiting for someone to join them. She didn't think much of it as they were about to leave until she noticed Meg's husband in the far right corner of the restaurant. He appeared as if he was with a male colleague, so nothing seemed suspicious from his end. However, she wondered if Jared purposely take them there to spy on Meg's husband.

"Hey, there's Mr. Wright. Let's go say hello," he suggested.

Kayla followed behind Jared on the way toward Mr. Wright. Jared seemed anxious to get over to his table, but Kayla couldn't figure out why. Mr. Wright wasn't doing anything wrong, but sitting with a man who appeared to be his age.

"Hello Mr. Wright, I was having lunch with Ms. McQueen and we saw you across the room. We just wanted to come and say hello."

"Oh, hi Kayla, how's Nicholas doing?"

"He's great, just getting smarter and bigger everyday."

"Yeah, that's what boys do. I'll see you guys around," Mr. Wright said, politely dismissing the two of them.

Kayla felt slightly odd as she walked back to Jared's car, but she didn't say anything. Kayla didn't want to continue to read too much into it, but Jared acted as if he had checked something off his list once he saw Mr. Wright.

"Did I miss something with Mr. Wright?" she asked.

"What do you mean?"

"Initially you said I asked to have this meeting, but in actuality, Meg called me and insisted that this was your idea.

Furthermore, we sat there the entire time and never discussed anything about my case. I understand that you have a deed with Meg, but I'm not trying to get involved in any twisted ordeal where someone is getting set up."

"Kayla, this whole ordeal is much bigger than you. I am your attorney for your case and there is nothing more to it. I apologize if I got side tracked and said things I shouldn't have, but I need you to stop trying to piece together a puzzle that you don't have a picture for," he demanded.

The remainder of the ride was an awkward silence. As Jared pulled around the office towards Kayla's car, he put the car in park and locked the doors.

"Listen, before you leave, I want to apologize. I didn't mean to get loud, but I am under a lot of stress that I can't discuss."

Kayla was visibly upset. She didn't ask to meet with him or for him to take her to lunch, but he had the nerve to talk down to her as if she was his kid.

"Kayla, I want you to understand that I'm just under a lot of pressure. As good as things seem, they really do get bad at times."

"I don't care about your problems, Jared, I'm just your client, remember?"

Kayla unlocked the door and got out of his car. As she drove away, she saw Jared watching her through her rearview mirror. She knew something was odd about this entire ordeal, but couldn't piece it together. She clearly knew he was a real deal attorney because the officers seemed to know him unpleasantly well at the precinct, and she saw his office with her own eyes.

Kayla was in a tough spot. She really needed an attorney for her case, so she couldn't turn him away. She had been dealing with the death of Dana for over five years and needed it to end. She had to play along, but at what cost? Meg was the one who recommended Jared, so she seemed to be the Queen of this chess game. Kayla wasn't sure if Meg cared about her so much that she would call on one of the best attorneys around to help her, free of charge. It was imperative to Kayla that she figured out Meg's motive, and what it was that Meg was gaining from the situation.

Chapter 8

It was the night of Meg's anniversary party and Kayla was getting her make-up done for the big occasion. Meg was the who's who of the town, so Kayla knew many rich and important people would be there. Although she was excited about the event, Kayla was feeling overwhelmed with life. She wasn't sure what Meg was trying to get her involved in, she continued receiving postponed court dates from the judge regarding the Dana case, and she was having frequent anxiety attacks from all the chaos. Along with everything else that was going on, she was also still busy making final plans for her own wedding day in less than two weeks. Her venue along with all the arrangements were set, her dress was scheduled to arrive in the next few days, Bryan had family he hadn't seen in years coming down, and four of his cousins, whom she never met, were Kayla's bridesmaids. To make matters worse, Michael, Nicholas's dad, had the nerve to leave her a threatening voicemail about joint custody of Nicholas. She figured he'd finally caught wind of her wedding and wanted to stir up strife, but he had no legitimate case since he was years behind on child support and hadn't seen Nicholas in over three years. With all the drama hanging over her head, Kayla was going to put it behind her for a few hours. She popped one of Dr. Roberts's miracle pills and she was ready for a night to remember.

Just as Kayla was walking out of the door, a man waiting outside standing beside a black limo startled her. Kayla looked around almost reluctant to approach him, but she figured he was at the wrong address and someone was missing his or her ride.

"Hello, are you Kayla McQueen ma'am?" he asked.

"Uhm…yes, I am, but I didn't request a limo, I'm sorry."

"Courtesy of Mr. Mancini," he said, opening the door.

Kayla looked inside and saw a bottle of champagne on ice along with a rose and a small card. She stepped into the limo and took a seat as the chauffeur immediately closed the door. It was almost as if he gave her no other option but to take the ride. She opened the note that read:

Hello Beautiful Lady,
I hope this isn't out of the
way, but Mrs. Wright gave me the address to send you transportation for
the big night.
I just wanted you to ride in luxury, as you deserve.

Kayla wasn't sure how she felt about the limo or the note. She didn't add Bryan as a guest since he told her he couldn't attend because of a work project, but what if he was home and got to the limo before she did? He surely would have assumed something was going on from another man sending his fiancée a limo, calling her beautiful, and what did he mean, "As you deserve"? Bryan didn't have his own law firm, but that ring on her finger and the home they were living in did him justice. How reckless of Meg to give this man her personal address! She decided not to call Meg just yet, but after the party, she would be sure to tell her how she felt.

Kayla arrived at the party and her medication had kicked in her system. She had forgotten about the heated conversation she was planning to have with Meg. She stepped out of the limo onto the red carpet in her shoulder-less, slimming black dress and a killer split that showed off her muscular calves. With her hair pinned up and a black diamond necklace to match her ensemble, she looked irresistible.

Kayla walked into the building as if she was the most dynamic woman in the room. She felt sexy, in-charge, and ready to flaunt herself in front of the rich crowd. She looked across the room and saw her gay friend Dexter, sitting at a table next to Meg's all exclusive entourage. She was on her way over to him until the photographer insisted he get photos of her. As she was working the camera, a familiar voice excitedly called her name.

"Kayla, stunning as usual!" proclaimed Mr. Wright, holding out his arms to embrace her.

"Hello to the most handsome man in the room," she countered back.

He laughed, "I can see why Meg adores you so much."

"It's definitely an honor to be here, Mr. Wright. You and Meg truly are an inspiration to me. I just pray that my marriage is as everlasting as yours."

"I'm sorry…your marriage?"

"Oh, yes, I'm getting married in two weeks. I was under the impression you were coming, you're definitely on the guest list as one of my priority guests."

"Oh, congrats and I'm sorry Kayla for my mundane reaction, but if you will excuse me, I have to call my attorney."

Kayla wasn't sure what was going on or why Mr. Wright's warm persona turned cold. It was almost as if her engagement bothered him, but Kayla knew that couldn't be it. Mr. Wright wasn't some creepy old guy who came on to younger women; he seemed to really love Meg. Kayla felt so liberated that she didn't bother to dig into it.

"Hey beautiful!" said Dexter as he flamboyantly stood up to hug her.

"Hey love, it seemed like it took me forever to get over here," she explained as she grabbed a wine glass from the waiter holding a tray.

"Honey, sit down…right now! I have a mouth full of "tea" to tell you."

"What else is new, boo, spill that "tea" right now," she urged.

"Well," he said, moving directly beside the chair she was sitting in, "so you know why the "curly sue twins" won't be attending, right?"

"I honestly didn't notice with so many people here, but why?"

"Girl, they got caught doing the nasty together in the supply room."

"GET OUT!" she yelled, almost too loud.

"Honey hush, yes they did. When I say they were going down, they were going down, girl."

"Wow, those little thots!"

"Hold on, boo, that's just the ice-breaker. Little Miss Tasha found out about the new pregnant nurse."

"What? How?"

"The story is, it got around to Tasha that her husband cheated with the nurse once, which we know is a lie, but any who, Tasha started overloading the girl with extra assignments and "accidentally" bumping into her in the hallways."

"Tasha is so petty and really needs someone to dust her trifling ass," Kayla implied.

"Girl yes, but when I tell you that this little nurse bitch ran up on Tasha with all her prenatal reports and paperwork with Tasha's husband's name on it, Tasha couldn't say shit. She told Tasha to 'read it and weep bitch' and the little nurse quit."

As they mischievously snickered and continued to talk about Tasha and the nurse, Kayla noticed Meg talking with a familiar face from across the room. She couldn't see exactly what was going on, but it appeared as if Meg and Jared were discussing something in private that they didn't want others to hear. They had their backs turned away from the crowd and they were noticeably isolated from everyone.

"No…this slut bitch, Francis didn't bring her side dude to this party. Hey Francis, you look stunning, girlfriend!" Dexter said, prancing over to another table. "Francis, who did your hair and makeup, girl, you look flawless! You are on one tonight, boo, and who is this person that you have on your arm, honey?"

Kayla shook her head as she watched Dexter greet one of their colleagues as if he didn't just call her a slut. She laughed hysterically as he continued to talk to Francis while turning around to her making faces behind Francis's back. He did it in only a hand language she could understand. Kayla turned her attention back to Meg who was now walking in her direction. Kayla was still excited from the pill and was happy to greet the woman of the hour.

"Excuse me boo thang, where are you finna go?" asked Dexter, returning to Kayla.

"Honey, didn't you just leave me like two seconds ago," she complained and snickered.

"You know good and well I had to check Francis in that curtain looking-ass dress she got on, honey."

"I guess it didn't help her to get a side dude then, huh?"

"Now girl, you know don't nobody want Francis, but her husband."

"Wait now, you just said-"

"Here comes your boss," Dexter whispered, leaning back crossing his legs.

"Kayla, I am so happy to finally see you, you look awesome!"

"I think we both know who this show belongs to," Kayla countered back, spinning Meg around and giving her a warm embrace.

"Hello Dexter, how are you sweetie?" asked Meg, oddly turning her attention to him.

"I'm good and I can tell by that smile you are as well, honey."

"Well, yes, it's the big ten, how could I not be."

"Yeah, how could you not be," he smugly replied.

There was an awkward silence as Kayla watched the intense stare between Dexter and Meg. Kayla knew that Dexter wasn't fond of Meg because of her bias views about gays. Dexter was convinced that Meg was a she-devil and only stuck to Kayla because she didn't want to come off as racist, too. Although Dexter was normally a friendly person, he could also be very judgmental. He was mixed with several different races, including black, and his mother was half-European. He encountered a lot of abuse from his white aunt, who he had to go stay with after his mother died from cancer. Meg didn't come off as racist to Kayla, so she felt that Dexter was judging Meg based on his experience with his aunt.

"Enough of the small talk with small people; I have million dollar guests to entertain. Kayla, I have to make a quick run home for a brief second. It seems as if I forgot my diamond bracelet and I feel naked without it. Could you come with me?"

"Uhm…sure," agreed Kayla, as she watched Dexter pretend to stick his hand down his throat as Meg walked off.

"Kayla, that bitch is rude and you need to watch your front and back around her," warned Dexter.

Kayla blew him a kiss and followed Meg to the Mercedes Benz that escorted her there. Just as she was walking out of the front lobby, Jared gently grabbed her arm and pulled her to the side.

"Wow, you look amazing, Kayla."

"Thank you, Jared; you don't look too shabby yourself."

"Look, I have something important I need to talk to you about, but I can't do it here."

"Is it about the case?"

"Well, I actually do have an update on that. They found Dana's cousin, Jessica guilty of killing Dana."

"What! Her own cousin?"

"There was DNA of someone's bloody fingerprint found on Dana's shirt as well as bloody skin cells under Dana's fingernails that were filed into evidence years back. Investigators knew that Dana put up a fight with the perpetrator, but they couldn't find any leads and were unable to find a DNA match since Jessica had never been in their database. Luck would have it that they were able to obtain samples of Jessica's DNA from her recent drug trafficking arrest."

"Wait, this is too much."

"I know, I didn't want to tell you all this here, but I may not get the chance to tell you what I have to tell you later. Is there anyway we can go somewhere and talk?"

"What about the grandmother and the little boy?"

"Listen Kayla, I shouldn't have told you that much, but I can't talk here. We can go to the coffee house right up the street if you would like. I promise that it won't take long."

Kayla was now skeptical of Jared, since he pulled that limo stunt at her home. She wasn't sure what his intentions were and he didn't come off as trustworthy. For all she knew he was trying to get photos of them being out together, so he could mail them to Bryan.

"Kayla, are you ready?" called Meg from the back seat.

"I have to go. I'll try to hook up with you Monday at your office," Kayla told him, walking away as if she was Cinderella.

The Mercedes quickly pulled off and Jared watched as if that was the last time he would ever see Kayla.

Once Kayla got in to join Meg, a glass of champagne awaited her. Meg seemed as if she was in the best mood of her life as she smiled and handed Kayla the glass. Kayla didn't want to spoil Meg's mood, but she had to ask her why she felt obligated to give Jared her address.

"Meg, I really do appreciate you getting Jared involved with my case, but I'm not comfortable with him having my address and leaving little "like" notes around my home that Bryan could've possibly found."

"Oh honey, Jared told me about the little crush he has on you, so I didn't think it would be a big deal if he sent you over a limo. I didn't know he was going to leave a little note. That was very unprofessional and I will address it with him later."

"So, when did he tell you about this "little" crush he has on me?"

"It was sometime after the lunch date you two had."

"Wait, we didn't have a lunch date. I went to the office to discuss my case and he said that he hadn't had lunch yet."

"Uhm…well, maybe it seemed like a date to him."

"Yet you still gave him my address after the fact."

"Kayla darling, don't blame me because you're beautiful. I just wanted to help you get the officers off your back, so I chose Jared. I knew no matter how serious the issue was that Jared would find a way to work it out for you. Do you know anyone else that could get you out of a double murder case?"

Kayla grew silent. No matter how much she didn't like the circumstances, Meg was right. She didn't know anyone in town who would be willing to help her free of charge. Besides, it wasn't that big of a deal, and she should have been enjoying the night instead of thinking about what could have happened.

"Yeah, I guess I am getting worked up for no reason. I guess it is kind of flattering to have a sexy attorney in lust with me."

"Well, he's never been with an African American woman before, so I think it's just a phase. Driver, leave the car running, we won't be long, dear." Meg said as she got out of the car.

Kayla felt some type of way about Meg's comment. How would she know whom that man has been with, and what makes her think it's just a phase? Was she trying to say a black woman could be no more than a fling to a man like Jared? Perhaps Dexter was on to something that Kayla had missed over the last year. Could Meg be jealous that the crush was on Kayla and not her? It sounded absurd in her mind considering the fact that Meg was married and Kayla was about to get married. Kayla remained in deep thought as she followed Meg towards her front door. She stood to the side as Meg put in her password. *Just like rich people to have passwords to a door*, she thought.

POW! A gun went off from the inside of Meg's home. Meg began to slowly fall backward with a startled look on her face.

Chapter 9

Kayla impulsively dived from the frameless elevated porch into the large batch of bushes that lined the front of Meg's home. She didn't know, or get the chance to see, who the shooter was or if the shooter even knew she was there, but her first instinct was to lie still and play dead underneath the bushes. Moments later, Kayla heard a car scrawl tires and quickly accelerate from the property. She suddenly realized that it must have been the chauffeur securing his survival and not worried if she and Meg lived or not.

"KAYLA, YOU GET BACK HERE!" yelled a man as he let off another round toward the vanishing car.

Obviously, the shooter was under the impression that Kayla had time to run to the car for a clean getaway, but what was more frightening was the fact that he let off another round as if he intended to shoot her, too. The man couldn't have seen her standing outside with Meg or else he would have seen her dive in the bushes, so how did he know she was even there. She heard a tremendous amount of scuffling, which made her assume that the shooter was moving Meg's body into her home. A few minutes later, she heard him slam the door shut.

Kayla was reluctant to move in fear that the man inside may hear her and come back to finish the job. Everything was dead silent. What felt like hours to her, was actually about ten minutes later when she heard the sirens from the police cars.

"Come out with your hands up!" they yelled, squatting behind the squad cars with guns in their hands.

Kayla refused to move. She was in fear they may mistake her for the assailant. After no response came from the home, two cops cautiously approached the door not noticing Kayla in the bushes.

"POLICE, OPEN UP!" they yelled, before finally busting the door open.

"Hey you, get your hands up!"

"I'm so sorry, Meg," cried the man from the front room.

Kayla suddenly realized that the man was Mr. Wright.

"Hey, someone get me an ambulance!" commanded the officer.

Kayla slowly came from the bushes as a third officer rushed over and demanded her to get her hands up. She complied in fear as she saw the chauffeur running from behind the police cars trying to explain what happened. They told him to get back as they proceeded to place Kayla in the back of the squad car. A minute or so later, the officers walked a sobbing, hand cuffed Mr. Wright from the home.

Kayla's attention turned back to the home where paramedics walked out Meg on a stretcher. She had an oxygen mask on her face, which clearly meant she was still alive. Kayla wasn't sure how to feel. She was relieved that Meg was still alive, but furious that whatever dirty little secrets Meg was holding could've gotten her killed.

Kayla knew there were only a few situations that would cause Mr. Wright to shoot his wife and that was infidelity or money, and they had plenty of money. She was hoping they would release her soon because she had to make it her business to get a hold to Jared. She knew he had something to do with this twisted situation.

After seeing the ambulance take Meg away and the cops take Mr. Wright off to jail, an officer came to the squad car and asked Kayla if she was okay and if she needed medical attention. She refused and after they recorded her statement, they offered a ride to her destination. The last thing Kayla wanted to do was ride in the back of a police car, so she refused their offer.

The runaway chauffeur then walked over and offered to take her back to the party. Although Kayla was a little skeptical, he did help her by calling the police and having the guts to return to the scene to explain what happened. With no other immediate options, she got into the back of the Mercedes and headed back to her limo.

She still couldn't believe the drastic turn the night had taken. She tried to call Bryan at least 12 times, but his phone kept giving a busy signal. This caused her even more anxiety worrying about his whereabouts.

"Hey ma'am, I'm sorry I had to leave you ma'am," spoke the Arabian chauffeur a few minutes into the drive.

Kayla didn't respond or even look up to meet his gaze from the front rearview mirror. She didn't know what to think. Did the chauffeur know something and was trying to get her to talk? All she knew was that she wanted answers as to why she was almost shot, and where in the hell was Bryan.

"I had to go get da' police, you know," he continued.

Kayla still didn't respond or even know what to say to him. All she could think about was the possibility of Mr. Wright coming outside to find her while his scary, self-serving ass drove off.

"I think anyone would have did the same thing, you know," he added.

As much as she hated to face the facts, this little dude was right. Had the circumstances been reversed and she heard a gun shot, she would have done the same thing. She wouldn't have risked being shot over some people she didn't really know, either. She wasn't even sure if she would have come back after calling the police.

"No hard feelings and thanks," she finally said to him.

Once they pulled up to the party, Kayla saw that the parking lot was still packed. Obviously, no one knew what just happened at the Wright's home. She didn't want to be the one to announce that the party was over because there would be too many people running up to her with questions. She also knew that when people did find out what happened, rumors would fly, and she would somehow become the center of the story. She was too overwhelmed to deal with it tonight. She had to find Jared. He would be the perfect person to disburse the crowd.

Kayla tried her best to mingle through the crowd as if nothing had happened. Although there were a few minor abrasions on her arms and shoulders from jumping in the bushes, her hair and everything else were in tact. Besides, as dim as the lighting was in the room, no one could really see details of anyone. Just as Kayla was about to give up her search, she spotted Jared in the front foyer.

"Excuse me, but I have something important to discuss with you in private," Kayla whispered, as Jared spoke guardedly on his phone.

Jared took a few steps forward and whispered something into his phone before ending the call.

"Oh, hey Kayla, how's the party?

"How's the party? Are you serious right now?" Kayla was getting aggravated. She could tell by his suspicious behavior that he knew something.

"Listen Kayla," he whispered, as he gently pulled her by her arm toward the side doors, "I know what you must be thinking and feeling, but it isn't what you think."

"How in the hell do you think you could possibly know what I'm thinking and feeling? Did you almost just get shot?"

"Please, lower your voice. No one can know what just happened. Meg is in the hospital and expected to have a full recovery. In the meantime, you have to act as if nothing happened."

"Now you listen to me rich boy. I want answers now or else I will tell everyone I know about your secret affair."

Kayla knew the only way to get him to talk was to test the waters and see if she could lie the truth out of him.

"You're bluffing," he challenged, trying to read her thoughts.

"Try me."

"You listen to me, Kayla. This is much bigger than the little knowledge in your brain that you think you have. I just kept your little ass from going to prison, so you owe me and you better respect that by keeping your little mouth shut."

"Oh, so that's how you feel. You helped a little black woman out on a case, so now I'm indebted to you. You know what, Jared; at the end of the day, I didn't kill or harm anyone, so the little circumstantial evidence the police had, couldn't have put me in jail even for one night, but oh, guess who is going to jail. That's right; your little bread and butter will be shacking up with the hard knocks after I become the key witness in this attempted murder case."

"What do you mean?"

"Jared, everyone knows that Mr. Wright is the real breadwinner of the two. While Meg may be a "star actress" per se, Mr. Wright owns the production. Without him and his connections, you'll lose half of your clients."

"You heartless bitch, you obviously should know what true love feels like. Why would you want to take him away from me?"

At that moment, Kayla came to a realization. Jared wasn't in love with Meg; he was in love with Mr. Wright! He must have been under the impression that Kayla knew about the affair with Mr. Wright opposed to the affair she was insinuating that he had with Meg. Then again, judging from the intense look of distress on his face, maybe he didn't care if she knew or not. Perhaps he was so tired of hiding his truth that he wanted to finally get it out and reveal it to someone. Anyone.

"I...I don't know how to respond," she finally said.

"Yes, I've been pretending with Meg, but I'm in love with Dylan Wright."

"Wait, you've been sleeping with them both?"

"There's no crime in sleeping with two people."

"It is when they're married."

"They're married, not me. Look, I had my reasons for being with the both of them, but all hell broke loose inside me when I saw Dylan with that other man at the restaurant. It brought about a jealousy that I never knew I had inside me."

"He looked like he was with an old colleague, what makes you think it was another lover?"

"That was the same old man that we met at a gay bar we went to a few weeks ago. The man invited us to one of his lavish house parties where he said he could introduce us to potential business aspects, but instead, when I turned my back, he tried to stick his tongue down Dylan's throat."

"But…But your sleeping with Meg so-"

"I don't love her and neither does Dylan, but this new guy is a whole new set of problems."

"Uhm…I'm almost sure that Meg lying in the hospital on a possible death bed is even more of a bigger set of problems."

"Kayla, you got to help me convince Meg that Dylan thought you two were burglars and he was protecting their home."

"So wait, you knew he was planning to shoot us?" Kayla asked, now fuming with anger.

"Of course, not! Listen, out of jealousy, I told Dylan I was interested in someone else. I tried to make him think it was you, but somehow he caught on to my deception and figured out it was his wife.

"So he shoots her instead of you, that's too fuckin' twisted."

"He loves me!"

"Well, clearly he must love her too if he was emotionally hurt enough to shoot her and sob all the way to the police station."

"What do you mean sob? He was emotional because I warned him about the money she was extorting from him to put in an off shore bank account for us."

"So wait…Meg is really in love with you and has no idea about you and her husband?"

"Kayla, I don't have to explain myself to you and frankly I don't have time to continue this mundane conversation."

"You're right, Mr. Mancini, you don't have to say another word. As a matter of fact, forget we ever had this conversation," Kayla said as she walked off. "Oh, I almost forgot, I'll call you from the hospital to let you know how Meg is doing."

"Kayla, I'm sorry. Listen, you're the only friend I have right now who knows the truth. Please don't abandon me in my time of need."

"That is the most selfish request you could ask right now."

"Do you want to know what's selfish, Kayla? What is selfish is the fact Meg asked me to take your case because it would be the perfect time to seduce you in your vulnerable state."

"What?"

"I didn't want to tell you this, but Meg asked me to take your case because she knew that Dylan was having suspicion about her possible infidelity."

"You mean you and her infidelity."

"Anyway, she came up with this so-called ingenious plan to get us off the hook.

When she learned of your situation, she figured it would be the perfect opportunity to capitalize on her scheme."

"There's no way I could be the perfect person because clearly, I have a fiancé that I live with and I'm about to marry."

"Kayla, she didn't care. She told me to handle your case because she knew I could get you off and by getting you off, you would feel like you owe me. We would become close enough for Dylan, as well as others, to assume we were lovers."

"That's the dumbest shit I've ever heard. There is no way that would have worked. Dylan and Meg had front row seats in my wedding."

"Meg doesn't care about marriage. Meg doesn't care if you or anyone else looks like a whore as long as she gets what she wants."

"So because you moved on to her husband, I'm supposed to get sucked into this monstrous picture you're painting of her, which I don't even know is the truth."

"Kayla, she sent that limo, wrote the note, and put my name on it. She said if your fiancé found out about me, that would make it that much better if he kicked you out, you lodged in one of the homes she offered you, and me show up to comfort you and you run into my arms. There are cameras set up in both homes. If all else failed and she had to consider a plan B, she was going to blackmail you into saying you were having an affair with Dylan for money or else she would show you and me together to your fiancé .

"She did freely offer me those condos with no questions asked, but how am I supposed to believe your lying ass and why am I so important in her love triangle?"

"You've been around her husband more than any other woman and everyone knows how much Dylan adores you, so if she could prove infidelity on him before he could prove it on her, then she could keep everything."

"But Mr. Wright is obviously gay, so how would people believe he was with me?"

"Are you serious, right now? We're not your average, flamboyant prototype. No one knows what we are and no one knows about us."

"That's it isn't it?"

"What?"

"You were tired of being his insignificant little secret, so in order for you to swindle your way out of being stuck with Meg, you made it your business to let Mr. Wright find out about your affair with her and the money, didn't you?"

"I didn't ask you to play detect-"

"Hey, you guys seen Meg and Dylan?" a guest asked, interrupting their quarrel.

Jared quickly escorted the guest back toward the crowd as if he had planned the intervention. Kayla wasn't about to wait for him to return and hear more of his half-truths. She needed to get to the hospital to see if Meg was alert and to see what input she could add to this bizarre circumstance. She ordered the limo that brought her there to take her home, so she could drive her own car to the hospital. In the meantime, she continued calling Bryan who never answered, nor returned her calls.

Chapter 10

Once the limo pulled up to Kayla's driveway entrance, she put her phone in her purse and proceeded to get out of the car. She thanked the driver for his services and instructed him to leave. Still feeling some type of way about Bryan's absence, she opened the garage only to see his truck parked beside her car. Kayla could feel her blood pressure raise that much more as she had a tense feeling that something strange was happening. She wasn't sure if she was still paranoid from the events that took place just a few hours ago, but she definitely felt the need to investigate. Bryan rarely, if ever, had anyone pick him up from the house. He definitely wouldn't purposely cut off access from her calls. She was almost afraid to go into the house, thinking there was a possibility that there was a burglar inside or even worse, finding Bryan lying hurt on the floor. Then, she thought that maybe Bryan figured she would be out with Meg all night, so he snuck a woman in their bedroom. *He wouldn't be that stupid*, she thought. She walked around the house to see if any windows or doors had been broken or compromised, but everything looked in tact. She decided to go through the garage that led into the kitchen. She figured she could swiftly run up the stairs through the kitchen to grab the locked gun from the closet.

With the gun in her hand, she tiptoed from room to room until she scoured the entire house. There was no sign of a forged entry, all of their household and personal items were in tact, but still no sign of Bryan. She locked the gun back in her closet and sat down on the couch in their master bedroom to try to figure things out. She remembered Bryan mentioning a bachelor party that Wayne was trying to throw, so maybe Wayne picked Bryan up while she was off to her shindig. Trying to stay calm and not overanalyze the possibilities, she still needed to see Meg. She hopped in her car and headed to the hospital in hopes that Meg was stable enough to give her some answers.

Kayla knew that the ambulance would likely take Meg to their hospital since she seemed to be in stable condition after the shooting. She hoped she wouldn't run into anyone from the party, but her chances were slim since a lot of people from the party also worked there. As she pulled up to the parking lot, she still had a nagging feeling about Bryan's absence but could only hope that her theory of him being with Wayne was accurate.

Kayla walked through the employee entrance of the hospital to avoid as many people as possible. She didn't see anyone sitting at the hall entrance desk, so she grabbed some charts to find out the location of Meg's room. She quickly dropped the charts and headed further down the hall.

"Honey, where have you been?" Dexter yelled, quickly walking up to her from the other end of the hall.

"Really Dexy, could you please be a little louder, please," Kayla sarcastically responded.

"Oh…no Miss Thang didn't, but anyway, I was worried about you. I couldn't find you after the commotion."

"You were so worried that you had time to go home and change your clothes and not call me, huh?"

"G-i-r-r-r-l, you are so snappy right now, but I understand, boo. How long did they hold you hostage?"

"What?"

"Girl, they said that you and Meg were held hostage until she jumped in front of the robbers and took your bullet and let you escape to get help. Is that true, girl?"

"Dexter, no, listen sweetie, this has probably been one of the longest nights of my life. Let me go talk to Meg and then I'll catch you up on everything later, okay?"

"Okay Boo, because you know I'll hold you down. Call me anytime if you need me, oh, except for after 1am because Troy is coming over and him need him some quality time."

Kayla deeply sighed as Dexter walked off. She lightly knocked on Meg's door and entered into her room. Surprisingly, Meg was sitting up and appeared to be reading something in her phone.

"Oh, hey honey, are you okay?" Meg asked, quickly closing her phone and reaching out to Kayla for a one-armed hug.

Kayla then knew that Meg must have been shot in the shoulder from the huge cast on her other arm.

"Oh no sweetie, don't worry about me, I came to see if you were okay. How are you feeling?" Kayla asked as she carefully embraced the hug.

"Well, to be honest, never in a million years did I think I would end up here on my anniversary night, but hell, I'm here."

Kayla could tell from the quiver of Meg's lips that she was about to burst into tears. Although Kayla had a slight sense of sensitivity toward Meg being shot, she still wanted answers. She needed to know how deeply involved had Meg gotten her into this messy situation and if she and her family were now targets. Kayla walked over, sat down on the edge of the recliner next to Meg's bed, and allowed her to finish grieving before she gave her the third degree. She knew it would only be a matter of minutes before Meg embellished on her innocence in the ordeal.

There was an awkward moment of silence as Kayla began to stare aimlessly around the room as Meg finished what sounded like her final sniffles. Kayla wasn't sure if Meg was waiting to see if she would get up and hold her hand as she cried those crocodile tears, but Meg clearly had another thing coming. It kept everything in her not to jump up and slap Meg for some of the things that Jared told her. Kayla knew she had to be calm and act as if she was on Meg's side in order to get some of the lies she knew Meg would tell and compare them to Jared's lies. Just like clockwork, she heard Meg let out a giggle as a conclusion to her crying episode.

"Oh God, can you believe we were almost killed over a stupid misunderstanding."

"What?" Kayla shockingly asked, giving her undivided attention to something that even she didn't expect Meg to say.

"I mean even I couldn't get drunk enough to believe my husband was a burglar, so how could he?"

Kayla bent down and put her head in her lap in order to continue to stay calm. Obviously, Jared had already convinced Meg to go with the burglar story in order to keep his lover out of prison. Kayla also realized that Meg clearly had no idea about her gay husband.

"So at what point did Dylan assume we were burglars? Was it the point when you put in your personal pass-code to your door or when he called my name and shot at me?"

"He was calling you to tell you he made a mistake," she fired back.

"How could you say that? Do you actually think that him letting off rounds of bullets at the car he assumed I was in was his way of saying he made a mistake?"

"You listen here young lady, I don't like your tone and I think it's time for you to leave. Nurse!" she yelled, pushing her call button.

"Are you sure you want to call another person in the room or would you like me to talk about your little lovers' offshore bank account that you have with Jared once the nurse comes in? Information around this hospital gets around very fast," Kayla said, challenging Meg.

"Yes ma'am, how can I help you Mrs. Wright?" The nurse asked, entering the room.

"Oh, I just need an extra pillow for my arm, please."

"You listen here, Kayla," Meg began, looking around at the door to make sure the nurse had exited, "I have been good to you and treated you like nothing less than a daughter, so don't sit here and turn your nose up at me."

"Meg, do you really think I give two flying fucks about you sleeping with Jared? My problem comes in when you're sending limos to the home where you know my fiancé and I reside. Then, I'm diving into bushes and dodging bullets. What makes you think I don't want to be around to raise my son?"

"Oh, for goodness sakes, Kayla, grow up! You act like you were actually hurt or sitting here in a hospital bed."

"That's not the fucking point, Meg!"

"Hey, you keep your voice down while you're in this room."

"Here's that extra pillow you requested," interrupted the nurse. "Is everything okay, Mrs. Wright?"

"Thank you, nurse that will be all." Meg rudely responded, without even looking at the woman.

"Listen Kayla, I know we're both emotional, but this will all be over very soon," continued Meg, after the nurse closed the door.

"Meg, this isn't a car accident where you simply exchange insurance information, file a report, and never see the person again. You're lying in a hospital bed from a gunshot wound by your husband, who is in jail."

"Thank you again, Kayla, for noticing the obvious, but like I said, everything will be okay, since I'm not pressing charges and my lawyer-slash-lover, as you put it, is ironing out the details."

Actually he'll be ironing your husbands shirts, thought Kayla.

"In the meantime, my dear, you will make sure you recant anything negative you've said regarding the shooting, and if asked, you will say since it was dark, Mr. Wright must've mistaken us for robbers, since he assumed we were at the party.

Kayla looked at Meg as if she was delusional, as she watched her struggle to pour herself a glass of water from a pitcher with her only good arm. She almost felt sorry that Meg thought she had the situation wrapped up in the palm of her hands, while not knowing that her side lover and husband were lovers, too. Since Meg clearly had no remorse for the drama she caused, Kayla decided to allow Meg to discover the truth about her husband on her own.

"I'm not changing a damn thing I've said and risk perjury charges for you. Good luck, Meg," she said, exiting the room.

"Oh Kayla, I almost forgot before you go. How is Bryan?"

"What's it to you?" she responded, turning around.

"Well, long story short, I asked Jared to do a little research just in case things get ugly. Did you have any idea your fiancé owned a very profitable business?"

"He has workers, but the company itself isn't his company."

"Oh, that's cute, so you don't know everything about Bryan."

"I would reckon I know more about my fiancé than you know about your husband of ten years, but that may be an understatement."

"Wow, shots fired! Well, here is a little history regarding your loving fiancé, Bryan. He and his roommate were thrown out of college for running a prostitution ring."

"Like I would believe you at this point, but if that did happen then obviously, it was thrown out of court since my fiancé doesn't have a criminal record. Have a great day and get that shoulder fixed."

"Kayla wait, you didn't allow me to get to the best part. Not only did they make thousands of dollars pimping women, but also their main hooker ended up dead. Let me know if you need Jared to reopen that case while my shoulder is healing, Sweetie."

Kayla walked out of Meg's room not knowing if she should believe anything Meg had told her about Bryan. He did roommate with Wayne back in college, and Wayne was definitely a well-known whore himself, but a prostitution ring and a dead woman? She had to know if there was any truth to Meg's claims, because if this was true and Jared reopened a cold case like this, she may not walk down the aisle at all.

Kayla's mind was racing with thoughts as she slowly walked back towards her car. She began to try and further recall some of the conversations she had with Bryan regarding his past. She definitely remembered him referring to himself as "wild" back in high school and college, but he never gave any specific details. She hated knowing that Meg possibly had something on her to blackmail her. She pulled her phone out of her purse and noticed that she had 11 missed calls. Just as she logged in to check the details, her phone rang again.

"Hello," she answered, unfamiliar with the number.

"Listen baby, I need for you to come and get me from the police station. I walked across the street to the pay phone because they confiscated my cell phone."

"Bryan, why in the hell are you at a police station?"

"I can't talk about this right now, just hurry and come get me. I'm in front of the shell gas station." He quickly hung up.

Chapter 11

Kayla was definitely out of her element after the phone call with Bryan. She couldn't understand how one night could progressively get worse as time passed. Meg had to have had something to do with Bryan being arrested. *"How could she!"* she thought aloud as she drove to rescue her fiancé. She was almost in tears thinking of how Meg could betray her even further than she already had. She was that much more sure that she wasn't going to change her story regarding the shooting. Not only was she going to repeat all the gory details about that night in court, she was also going to give the motive of why Mr. Wright wanted to shoot his wife. She knew she needed proof, so she was going to have another meeting with Jared and pretend to take his side, so she could record him admitting to the affairs. To stir up even more strife, she also had it in her mind to play the recorded tape in front of Meg while she was laying in her hospital bed from taking a bullet for someone who she thought loved her.

Once Kayla arrived at the phone booth, Bryan quickly spotted her car and hopped in the passenger side. He slid his seat back and put his hood over his head as if someone was looking for him. It suddenly dawned on Kayla that he clearly hadn't been arrested unless someone already bailed him out before she arrived. She had never seen Bryan so distraught, so she knew that whatever reason he was down at the precinct had to be pretty serious.

The ride home was silent as Kayla allowed him to collect his thoughts before her asking him questions. She pulled into the driveway of their home, cut off the car, and didn't even bother to open the garage. She wasn't sure what he was about to tell her, so she mentally tried to prepare herself for a worst case scenario. After a few minutes of extra silence, he lifted his seat as he grabbed her hand and kissed it.

"I figured my past would come back to bite me, but I thought the Mrs. Jenson situation was my punishment. I thought if I made things right on that and prayed for forgiveness that I wouldn't have to suffer for any more wrong doings."

"Bryan, you are scaring me. What exactly are we dealing with where the police would even legally be allowed to keep your personal belongings if you're not arrested?"

"It all started when Wayne wanted to take me to some strip club for his surprise bachelor party that he called himself getting together. For some reason tonight, I really wasn't in the mood to see any strippers, so I told him lets go to a bar and chill. On the way to the bar, we got stopped by the police and this idiot had weed and a concealed weapon in the car."

Kayla was actually relieved when Bryan told her what happened. She was wrong about Meg having anything to do with it. Bryan being arrested was just a coincidence to that night's events. Obviously, the car had to be registered in Wayne's name, so Wayne would own up to the weapon and the weed. Even if Wayne didn't own up to it, she would agree to side with Jared's story about the shooting in exchange for Jared agreeing to act as Bryan's attorney, and get Bryan out of this minor incident.

"Well baby, don't worry about it. It sounds minor and I have an attorney that will relieve you of any weed or gun possession charges."

"Oh my God, Kayla, stop thinking you can fix every damn thing. Do you really think I would be worried about some stupid ass weed charges? This shit is way bigger than that."

"Okay, well, fill me in on this big ass problem that I can't help with," Kayla remarked, now even more aggravated.

"Listen, let's just go in the house, chill out, and we can talk about this tomorrow."

"You know what, Bryan. I was trying to listen to you and be understanding to your situation, but as usual, you took me to another level. I almost got my head blown off by a cheating gay husband, so right now isn't the time to blow me off!" she yelled.

"What the hell are you talking about, Kayla."

"I will get to that later. Right now, I need you to tell me what the fuck else we're dealing with, so we can figure out a way to resolve it."

"Well," he began as he cleared his throat, "Wayne and I stayed in a campus apartment together back in college. We both had a few friend girls that were promiscuous, but we were all just college students trying to get by without having to get a regular job. We all mutually came up with an idea to introduce the girls to rich college boys that had a hard time meeting girls and who couldn't get dates. Long story short, the message got around that we were matchmakers, so we began charging fees to the guys and girls for hooking them up with one another."

"So...you were pimps?"

"Stop being so judgmental, no we weren't pimps. We never told the girls to have sex with these guys, nor did we tell the guys to expect sex from the girls. We just simply introduced two people who probably wouldn't have met under normal circumstances."

"Okay, still sounds like a low grade of prostitution without strictly enforcing it."

"Look, if two consenting adults wanted to have sex after meeting, that isn't against the law. I personally don't know or didn't ask the guys or girls what happened after they met."

"Whatever Bryan, but I do not understand what's so wrong about these "innocent" transactions. What does this have to do with the current day and time?"

Bryan took another deep breath, "Although Wayne did have a permit for his gun, he was still fingerprinted for having the weed. His fingerprint came back as a match for an ongoing investigation from an unsolved cold-case file. At least that's what the officer claimed."

"What was the unresolved case?"

Bryan put his hands on his head as if he didn't even believe what he was about to say. "Baby, they think Wayne had something to do with a girl that was killed back then."

"Wait, you mean one of the girls that you two introduced to the guys?"

"Not really, see, she was a roommate of one of the girls who worked for us. She invited herself into the mix. I never met her, but Wayne told me about her. He said she was sexy and would bring in a lot of money. I told him I don't deal with outside women, so he was the only one who dealt with her."

"Did one of the guys kill her or something?"

"I don't know. All I know is that someone gave the police my name and left Wayne out the entire ordeal. Wayne wasn't mentioned at all during the course of the investigation, and I wasn't about to snitch him out. I knew they didn't have anything on me, so afterwards, I assumed the case was dropped."

"Did Wayne ever question you?"

"Why would he question me?"

"I would think as your business partner and roommate that he would be concerned whether or not his name was mentioned, or if they were coming to question him, too."

"I really don't recall him saying anything at all. I just don't understand how all these fucking years later they would have his fingerprint. I'm sure a lot of guys were in that girl's apartment."

"Well, Wayne didn't have a record. I mean, he clearly is an asshole, but he isn't a killer...Is he?"

"Of course not, Kayla...I don't think."

"Where is the doubt coming from?"

"What doubt?"

"If you say 'I don't think so' then there's obviously something that makes you look at him a different way, Bryan."

"I don't know, Kayla, damn!"

"I'm on your side, babe. Do you remember something he may have said?"

"Kayla, I really can't tell, okay. I mean, Wayne has always had a negative demeanor about women, but I always figured it was because his mom had abandoned him when he was around five or six."

"Have you ever known him to hit a woman?"

"No, and he seems like he is completely in love with Jesse, so when they told me-" he abruptly stopped talking.

The car was silent and Kayla could tell that Bryan was about to confess something that was disturbing. She grabbed his hand and allowed him to gather his thoughts. Kayla didn't know who Bryan was referring to as "they", but she wanted to prevent Bryan from feeling like he was back in the interrogation room.

"Baby it's just me. You know what we talk about doesn't leave this car. Go ahead and tell me what they told you."

"The police said that the dead girl was named, Justice Dame."

Kayla was bewildered. She had no idea whose name Bryan just said, but it had to be someone he knew. She still didn't ask him any questions, but looked at him as if she was ready for some answers.

"Justice Dame is Jesse's sister."

"No Bryan, this is crazy. There's no freakin' way Wayne could pull something like that off. Who told you she was Jesse's sister?"

"Well, Wayne did. He would complain to me that Jesse talks about her dead sister all the time, so when the police mentioned an old case and said the girl's full name, I knew it was Jesse's sister."

"Bryan, this has to be a coincidence. There is no way Wayne would be having sex with this girl knowing he killed her sister."

"No one said he killed her, they just said his fingerprints were found at the scene. He could've been with someone, dropped that guy off at her apartment, and left."

"Well, why wouldn't he turn that person in?"

"Maybe he felt like he would've been an accessory to the crime for dropping the guy off at Justice's apartment. I don't know, Kayla. I'm just as confused as you."

"But still there would have to be daily guilt whenever he looks at Jesse's face knowing that he may know her sister's killer."

"Perhaps the car, house, and other things he's buying for them is compensation for the guilt, Kayla, I do not know. All I know is that my nigga is in jail regarding a pending murder."

After a few minutes of rethinking the times she had been around Wayne, Kayla finally pulled into the garage and followed Bryan into the kitchen as he immediately grabbed whiskey from the cabinet. He took a few shots and blankly stared at the floor as if he was trying to recall something that may jog his memory. Although Bryan said he was cleared of any charges, she wondered if Bryan knew more than he led on, but she dared not to ask him.

Morning came quick as the rising sun hit Kayla's face through the open blinds. Bryan was already up looking out the window as if he was waiting on someone. She wasn't sure if he slept at all, since it had only been a few hours since they lied down.

"Good morning babe, I didn't mean to wake you," he said, walking over to the bed to kiss her on the forehead.

"It's okay, I didn't sleep well anyways."

"I'm going to go shower and then go take care of a few things, okay?"

"Okay, I'm going back to sleep," she said, rolling over.

"Okay...hey, wait, what is with this shit about a gay man and a bomb you were talking about last night?"

"What? No, I said-"

"*Ding dong*," interrupted the doorbell.

"Who is at our door this early in the fuckin' morning?" asked Bryan.

"I don't know, babe, do you want me to get the gun?"

"Hell no, Kayla, what if it's the police?"

Bryan followed Kayla to another bedroom to look out the window facing the front of their house. They couldn't see who it was at the door from their angle. Kayla looked toward the street and recognized the car parked out front.

"Wait, isn't that Jesse's car?" she asked.

The doorbell rang again. Only this time, it was continuous and rapid, and then a forceful banging followed.

"Bryan, I need to talk to you, it's urgent," yelled Jesse from outside.

Chapter 12

Hearing Jesse's voice at the door definitely confirmed it was who Kayla assumed it was outside their home. Kayla became infuriated at the fact that Jesse would come to their house that early and address only Bryan as if she didn't exist. She didn't check Jesse the last time she was over their house and on some disrespectful shit, but at that moment, Jesse clearly had the right one.

"Now, I know good and got damn well this trash isn't banging on my door like she pays bills in this muthafucka."

"Kayla, please calm down. We don't know what kind of information she's gotten from the police, so let's at least try to be understanding."

"We don't owe her any fuckin' explanations. No one told her to go fuck two best friends. I know you don't think for one second I'ma pull out a got damn sympathy card after what I saw in your secret whore box."

"Kayla, anything that did or did not happen was before I even knew you existed. Are you fuckin' kiddin' me right now, after what I've been through last night?"

Kayla saw the sincerity in Bryan's eyes and calmed down. He was right. Whatever happened between him and Jesse was years ago before they met when he was being the typical college boy. Bryan was good to her, so it wasn't him that she didn't trust, it was the cunt outside. She kissed him softly on the cheek and went downstairs to the door. She opened it and saw a crying Jesse with smeared mascara all over her face.

"You listen here. I'm going to allow you to speak to my fiancé, but if you ever come on my property again yelling and beating on my doors, I will put two bullet holes in both your legs. This is not a threat. It's a promise."

Kayla shut the door in Jesse's face as Bryan reopened it behind her. He wasn't sure if the horrified look on Jesse's face came from Kayla's threat or information about Wayne.

"Uhm...how can we help you, Jesse?"

"Wayne is in jail and you're the only person I can talk to," she whimpered, beginning to cry again.

"Uhm...," he looked back to be certain Kayla had stepped away, "You can have a seat on the couch."

She slowly walked in as Bryan closed the door behind her. He turned on the television, but made sure the volume was low. He wasn't sure what to say as he sat down on the sofa that was adjacent to the loveseat where Jesse was sitting. He decided to wait until she spoke before making any statements. Moments later, Kayla came downstairs with a leopard handbag and sat at the end of their chaise lounge chair that was across from Jesse.

"Maybe I should go," Jesse said, getting up from the couch.

"Wait a minute, Kayla, what are you doing?" Bryan asked.

"Oh, I know she didn't think I was going to allow her to talk to you alone, did she? No, she came here to talk, so she'll be talking to us."

"Kayla, what's with the bag?" Bryan asked, pointing to it. He was bothered by the suspicious way she was carrying it.

"Babe, I was about to put my face mask on and put my rollers in my hair," she playfully gestured.

"I first want to apologize for my behavior a minute ago," Jesse began as she sat back down and looked at Bryan who seemed content with Kayla's response, "I know beating on your door was a little dramatic, but I'm at a loss."

Bryan knew since Jesse wasn't Wayne's wife, the police wouldn't give her too much information. Bryan still felt some type of way about how Jesse acts every time she's at their home, so he didn't have much respect for her either, however, he did sympathize with her about her sister and what he said to her the last time she was there.

"I woke up around four this morning and realized Wayne wasn't there. His phone was off, so I called his dad to see if he may have crashed there. His dad said that he got arrested and we could go bail him out Monday morning."

Kayla wasn't buying the innocent role this chick was playing. She knew that Jesse had more information than what she was leading them to believe. She looked over at Bryan who clearly wasn't buying it either. Kayla was ready for this broad to get the hell out of their house.

"Okay, so let me get this straight. You pounded on our door just because your guy went to jail on the weekend and can't get out until Monday?"

"No, I beat on Bryan's door, because I want to know why my man is in jail, when Bryan was the last person he was with."

"Yeah, we were together but-"

"What we're not going to do is act like Bryan is the only one in this room," Kayla said, interrupting Bryan in mid sentence.

"According to Wayne, Bryan was the one who bought this house and is the one who has information about my man, so as far as I'm concerned, he is the one who I will address."

"Okay, this is about to get out of hand so, Jesse, I'm going to need for you to-"

"You listen here you dusty bitch, I don't give a fuck if Wayne himself bought this muthafuckin' house. I am the head queen in charge of this bitch and no low class ass opportunist is about to disrespect me in my shit," Kayla argued, rising from her chair. Bryan quickly restrained her.

"Jesse, its best you leave and wait until Monday to talk to Wayne," suggested Bryan.

"All I want to know is how my man ended up getting arrested, when he was trying to show you a good time before marrying this lame ass broad."

"Jesse, step the fuck up out of our house right now before shit gets ugly."

"You two are some fuckin' losers and Bryan, I faked every time we fucked," Jesse said, walking towards the front door.

"While you're at it bitch, ask your man why he's being investigated for your sister's murder, whore."

"Ahh...Kayla, no." Bryan said, putting his head down, still restraining her.

"You lying bitch!" screamed Jesse, running towards Kayla as Bryan quickly turned her around to protect her.

"Bryan, let me go!" yelled Kayla.

Bryan pushed Kayla on the chair as he backed into a wall in order to get Jesse off his back. Jesse began swinging wildly as Bryan grabbed her hands, but not before she connected her fist with his head, hitting him on the side of the ear. Bryan let her arms go and instinctually grabbed his ear from the sharp pain he felt against his face. Jesse's keys had cut him. Kayla came in from the side with a solid hit and decked Jesse on the jaw, making her fall to the floor. Jesse, startled by the blow, scooted toward her purse as if she had something in it to use. Kayla quickly grabbed her leopard bag, pulled out her pink 9mm pistol, and pointed it at Jesse.

"Bitch, you got two seconds to get ya' dusty ass up and out of our house."

"You're gonna pay for lying, Kayla," threatened Jesse, crawling off the floor and lifting herself up with help from the door.

They watched Jesse stumble off and get in her car to make sure she didn't try to pull anything. Kayla closed and locked the door as Bryan went upstairs to the bathroom mirror to observe his wound. Kayla shortly followed behind with a damp towel and some peroxide to help. It was a minor cut from his ear to his jaw line, but it didn't appear as if it needed stitches.

"Kayla, why did you tell that girl that Wayne killed her sister?"

"No, I said he was being investigated for her murder."

"That's not the point, Kayla. You know she's going to run back and tell Wayne that we said he killed her sister."

"I don't give a fuck what she runs back and says. If he knows he's innocent, he should just laugh at it."

"Kayla, be realistic. No one is going to laugh about being involved in a murder case. For all I know, this psycho broad is going to bring me in this shit."

"OHH…I get what this is about. You don't want Wayne to find out you fucked his whore behind his back."

Bryan turned around from the mirror and leaned against the counter. He knew Kayla's adrenaline was still on ten from what just had happened, so he took mercy on her. Arguing with his fiancée was the last thing he needed.

"Kayla, I don't want Jesse now and I didn't want her back in college. The truth is, a girl that I was involved with around that time was being an asshole and Wayne was being an asshole, too about this mystery girl. One thing led to another, I fucked Jesse, and that's the truth. What you have to learn is to stop making everything about you and eliminate small situations that could become detrimental."

He kissed her on the forehead, left from the bathroom, and began to put on his clothes. Kayla watched him as she thought about what he said. Bryan was right. What if Jesse would have tried to pull out a gun too and caused Kayla to shoot her, or what if Jesse shot Kayla or Bryan first?

It made no sense that she was bugging out about a woman he dealt with years ago, but what Bryan didn't understand was that she wasn't going to allow any woman to disrespect her in their home.

"So let me get this straight, I was supposed to allow her to disrespect me in our home?" Kayla asked, standing beside the bathroom door.

"Kayla, why did you come back downstairs in the first place?"

"What do you mean? I wanted to see what she had to say."

"Kayla, you and I both know you came downstairs with your little bag with the hopes or intentions for something to pop off. Not because you thought that the girl was a serious threat, but because you didn't like the thought of me fucking her years ago."

"Okay, so you would allow me to be alone in our house with a guy you know I slept with years ago."

"If Nicholas's dad was in his life, I guess I wouldn't have a choice, would I?"

"She's not your baby momma!"

"No shit, but she's my nigga's woman, so that's just some shit we have to deal with until he stops fucking with her or I stop fucking with him. The end."

Bryan went downstairs, grabbed his keys and left. Kayla knew that if the roles were reversed that Bryan would be just as involved, if not overly involved, as she was. Speaking of which, with all the chaos going on she had forgotten all about the threatening voicemail that Michael left her regarding Nicholas.

Not only did she detest this man for abandoning Nicolas, but also she knew if Michael started showing up all of a sudden, Bryan would think it was Kayla trying to get some type of revenge from the Jesse situation. Kayla needed this small problem to disappear. There was only one person who was dirty enough and had the right amount of pull to make this happen. She decided that she would go visit Jared Monday morning at his office.

Kayla didn't get the chance to talk with Jared as she intended since Bryan's cousins, her bridesmaids, came in town that next day. Bryan took the time to catch up with his family as she took the time to get to know them. Much to her surprise, his cousins were supportive and easy to accommodate. Their wedding was two weeks away, and more of Bryan's family trickled in throughout the week. Only two of Bryan's cousins stayed at their home. Kayla noticed Bryan's face lit up as if he was a kid from being around his family. Having them around temporarily made him forget about his situation with Wayne, which also made Kayla subside her issues. She was on her first week of her four-week leave from work, so life seemed to be stress-free the last few days.

Later in the week, Kayla decided to do something special for her guests. She decided to check her bank to see how much she had in her budget to take the ladies shopping. Kayla's heart nearly fell out of her body when she saw she had an extra $100,000 in her account. She assumed the bank had made a mistake until she checked her transactions and noticed that the deposit came from the hospital like her normal checks. She knew this had to be another one of Meg's scandals that just might take the cake.

Chapter 13

Kayla didn't want Bryan's cousins to get suspicious about anything, nor did she want to come off as if she was hiding something, so she took them shopping anyway since she had already told them she would. Even though the ladies knew that Kayla was trying to be gracious and hospitable, they rejected her offer to buy the items they picked out. Instead, they practically forced Kayla to accept some earrings they had picked out and purchased for her.

Later that night, after Bryan arrived home, Kayla told him and her guests that she had a few errands to run. Although she wasn't 100% sure, Kayla knew that the money in her account had to have had something to do with Meg wanting her to say what she needed her to say about Mr. Wright. It had to be a lot of money at stake in order for them to be able to shell out the amount they gave her. Although the funding appeared as if it came from the accounting department at the hospital, Kayla knew that this was a part of Jared and Meg's elaborate scheme. This situation was nothing short of embezzlement and Kayla was that much more pissed that they volunteered her into something she didn't ask them to give her. In addition, it angered her that she had to go find them first in order to address the matter.

"Hey Kayla, how are you sweetheart?" Meg asked, answering Kayla's call.

The last thing Kayla wanted to do was talk to Meg. She had drove around Jared's office in hopes to catch him before he left, but no one was there. She called his phone several times, as she continued to drive around the general area, hoping he would eventually pick up, but he didn't. She knew she was down to her last option when she called Meg. Kayla had already heard from Dexter that they discharged Meg from her hospital bed a few days earlier, so with unforeseen cash flow in her account, Meg would obviously make herself readily available to explain whatever immoral venture she had in mind.

"Look, I need to speak with you and Jared as soon as possible. I know that you two knew it was only a matter of time before I made the discovery in my account."

"Oh, okay. Well, you're more than welcome to come by my house, Hun."

"Oh no...I don't need a repeat episode of what happened the last time."

"Well, I suggested my house because Jared is actually here now going over some litigation documents, and I'm not sure the next time we'll both have time to meet with you."

After finally agreeing to meet them at Meg's home, Kayla had a gut feeling this was a terrible idea. If Jared was actually at Meg's home, they both clearly knew she was calling him. She could imagine the bitch saying 'don't answer, make her call me'. She had to think of a clever diversion just in case it was a setup.

"Hey Kayla, I missed you so much," said Meg, opening the door.

"Look, I know our last conversation didn't go so well, but I'm not here to argue, I just want clarity. Besides, I told my fiancé I was coming over to visit you since you were released from the hospital and he threatened to come get me if I wasn't back in 15 minutes," Kayla explained, walking in the corridor.

The truth of the matter was that Kayla didn't tell Bryan where she was going. She led him to think she was doing something for the wedding. Kayla didn't want him to know the whole truth because he would have rejected the idea of her going over, since she told him what went down the night of the shooting. He actually wanted her to quit her job, but he knew she was too independent and passionate about her work. Kayla's objective was to make it seem as if Bryan knew where she was, just in case they tried something funny.

"Wow Kayla, I'm not that awful, am I?"

"You sent a lover's note and a limo to my home from your "mister" in order to damage the marriage I have planned, I almost got shot because of your infidelity, and now you want me to lie and say it was all a misunderstanding. No, you're not awful, you're horrible."

"Well, aren't we being honest and judgmental."

"Meg, where did the money in my account come from?"

"Kayla, I'm sure you can consult with your bank regarding any transactions that are in your account."

"I didn't drive over here against my fiancé's wishes so that you can be with the bullshit.

You and I both know you had something to do with the extra $100,000 in my account. I need to know where this money came from and what terms and conditions you expect me to follow."

"Yes, that's the Kayla I know and love. I knew you would come around, and let's be honest; money has always been and will be the greatest motivational tool. We are in this together, and we help build one another up to succeed."

"As confusing as it may have sounded, I know what I said may have seemed as if I was on board, so let's be clear about my position on the matter. I haven't agreed to anything yet, until I know where this money came from and what you two assume, or should I say intend, on asking me to do for this dirty payoff."

"You talk as if you're above $100,000 and you don't have a wedding coming up, a son to take care of, and a fiancé who works 20 hours a day to bring home the bacon."

"Listen, I didn't ask you to analyze neither my finances nor my family life. To be perfectly honest with you, we got what we have without this unplanned nonsense you seem to be calling a favor instead of a fraud."

"It will only be a fraud if you refuse the money, sweetie."

"What?"

"I knew how ethical you would try to be regarding the whole situation, so I had to put some ties to it. Every year we pick someone in financial need, such as single moms like you, to aid in their financial growth. Since you're not married and there is no record of Bryan existing in any of your personal finances, I was able to choose you since I am the chairperson of the organization."

"Why would you do that when you know there are mothers out there that really could use and need this money?"

"Uhm…that's not my problem, Dear. So, as I was saying, if you choose not to comply with our setup, I have records that indicate you are the second chairperson to handle the affairs of the organization if for some reason I am incapacitated. Since I was in the hospital for a few days because of the shooting, it would only make sense that you greedily decided to put the money in your own account while poor old Meg was down and out."

"That's almost smart, but stupid. Why would I put a traceable $100,000 into my account?"

"Who said it was traceable? Now, stop trying to over think me and thank me."

"I'm not thanking you for being a conniving crook."

"Oh, yes you are, ma'am. You're going to write a letter to the foundation about how happy and thankful you are to be a recipient of the funds."

"You've clearly lost your mind if you think I'm going to help you with your scheming. You and Jared might as well forge that letter like you forged those documents of me being a second chairman for a foundation that I never knew existed."

"Okay then, take your little ass to jail, Kayla, but ask yourself are you really hearing yourself. I am allowing you to decide your own fate between staying wealthy to get rich or end up back on welfare."

"What!"

"Yeah, that's right, Kayla. I got Jared to dig up a little background about you, Ms. McQueen. Turns out you were getting food stamps on the government assistant program about three years ago. In addition to you being in poverty, you had to go get yourself involved in a murder case regarding your roommate, and then there's the fact that Nicholas's biological father is a drug dealer. When people see you, sweetheart, that's how they'll see you. Who do you think they will believe when shit hits the fan? Do you think they will believe me, a rich, upstanding head administrator of the nursing department, who does countless charitable events or you, a single mother from the ghetto who will do anything not to go back?"

"There's a place in hell for you, Meg."

"Oh Kayla, must we bicker and argue about everything as if we're an old, married couple? This is a simple situation to take advantage of and become the woman you've dreamed of becoming. You and I both know it would take you years to save up what I gave you in an hour."

"I've never asked you for anything and don't need your handouts. I am going to forward the money in a check right back to you, and I don't want any part of this," Kayla said, walking towards the door.

"Well, you know…I could just shoot you."

"What did you just say to me?"

"I said there is the option of doing away with you, Kayla."

"Bitch, if you ever in your life try to threaten me again, I will take that antique sword you have hanging on your wall and shove it up-"

"Uhh…Meg, I uhh…I uhh…think you need to come outside…uh…just for a minute," stuttered Jared, bursting through the French doors of the living room and interrupting Kayla as she was pointing her finger in Meg's face.

"Oh Jared, you are just in time," Meg nervously said, "I was hoping you were finished with that project, so you can join the conversation Kayla and I were having about the great opportunities we were offering her."

Kayla wasn't paying any attention to Meg. Her eyes were fixated on Jared. She hadn't ever seen him so distraught. He looked horrific. He had sweat all over his face, his clothes were muddy, and there was a scratch from his nose to the top of his forehead.

"Uhm, Jared sweetie, did you fall back there on the concrete or something?" Meg asked, walking over to observe the injury.

Jared just stood there and didn't say a word. It was almost as if he was lifeless by the way he was standing with his arms loosely swinging to his sides. Kayla began to regret she came over.

"Meg, I need you to come outside," Jared finally spoke.

"Okay, did you need me to grab you guys some coffee or wine while you iron things out?"

"That's the thing, Meg, she's gone," explained Jared.

"Oh, she already left? Okay, well, since you're done with her, we can go ahead and wrap things up with Kayla."

"Meg, I just told you I am leaving and to count me out of your treacherous ploy," said Kayla.

"I NEED EVERYONE IN THIS GOT DAMN HOUSE TO COME OUTSIDE RIGHT NOW!" Jared yelled in a devious tone.

Kayla and Meg both looked at one another with a slight sense of fear from Jared's rant. Deep down inside, they knew whatever he wanted to discuss outside wasn't good. Although Kayla was ready to leave, she was extremely curious to know who the mystery woman was that they were trying to drag in their web of deception. Kayla had the feeling that Meg was trying to keep whatever she and Jared had going on in the backyard between them, but Jared wasn't having it. Kayla figured Meg and Jared were both embarrassed that this mystery woman wasn't buying into whatever Jared was selling either. Jared probably threatened the woman, in return, she cursed him out, and a physical altercation likely ensued that the mystery woman obviously got the best of, and then she escaped.

They slowly walked behind Jared toward the back patio that led to the swimming pool and the artificial waterfall. Kayla could see several papers scattered on the ground and on the table of the extravagant outside furniture set Meg had next to the swimming pool. As they walked around to the far side of the patio furniture by the fence, Kayla gasped with her hand over her mouth. There was no way she was seeing what she saw in front of her.

"Uhm, Jared my dear, what's going on?"

"This is what I've been trying to tell you," he said.

"Yeah, but why is Gabby lying face down in the grass?" Meg asked.

Chapter 14

Kayla stared in horror as she hoped this was a bad dream, while Gabby's lifeless body lay in front of her. She felt like she was outside of her body watching herself in a movie or a play. She was waiting on Gabby to move her fingers, roll over, or any type of movement that would indicate she was still alive. Nothing happened as silence devoured the moment.

"Maybe one of you guys can try to give her CPR or something, I mean, you are nurses, right?" Jared finally suggested with his hands on his head.

"Sweetie, you don't give CPR to a dead person. Kayla, do you want to try?" Meg condescendingly asked.

"You couldn't pay me an extra $200,000 to touch her."

"I am glad you brought that up, honey. We need to go back in the house and further discuss what Kayla needs to do in order to keep us all covered."

"Meg, have you lost your fucking mind? This shit clearly tops priority of what we have to discuss with Kayla."

"Okay Jared, let's get something straight right now. I need you to not ever swear at me again, and put on your big boy pants. Stop being so dramatic, go wrap Gabby's ass in plastic, and put her in your trunk. You can dump her ass off in the woods later."

"I'm not putting her in my Lexus!"

"Why not, it's not like she's bleeding. From the looks of it you did a pretty clean kill."

"Hey, this was an accident! Don't make it seem like I'm some monster who does this professionally. This is just as much as your fault as it is mines, Megan."

"You wait a minute Mr. Attorney at Law. When I left you two outside, I told you to talk to her and make sure any information that she had disappear, not to make her disappear with it."

"Well, had you stayed out here, Megan, you would have known she wasn't compliant and threatened to blackmail us with recordings and videos of us."

"Wait, you killed a girl who has recorded evidence lying around, only God knows where, of things we've said and done?"

"Meg, I'm not an idiot? Of course, I got all of that information before things got out of hand."

"Okay, so just how did things get out of hand, Jared?"

Jared looked at Meg, then at Kayla, and then back at Meg who had her arms crossed waiting on an answer. He had no response to how Gabby was on the ground because he hadn't thought the lie through. Kayla began to believe that there were no recordings.

Gabby must have had information about Jared sleeping with Meg's husband and threatened to tell Meg. It was the only thing that Kayla could think of that he couldn't say.

"You know what, Jared; we'll talk about this later. I'm going to go get some plastic from the storage room; you can take Dylan's pick-up, and dump her off."

"I'm not putting her body in his truck either."

"Oh my freaking goodness, why are you being such a diva today? What other solution do we have?"

Life had taken such a drastic turn in so little time. Kayla couldn't figure out the exact point where her decisions caused a domino effect of bad karma. Perhaps it was the day she decided to keep her lead position at work by embellishing what she told Meg about Gabby, or it could have been what she did to Jesse. Perhaps bad karma came from the plans she decided to make in order to terminate the custody issue with Nicholas's dad, but everything was falling apart.

After temporarily leaving the argument, Meg came back with a roll of plastic and put it beside Gabby's body. Kayla stood there still in shock as they argued back and forth about the end plan. It was so surreal that she continued to stare at Gabby, hoping she would move. *Move Gabby move. I know you can do it*, she thought. How could something she embellished about Gabby coincidentally turn out to be far deeper than the truth? As the sky began to mysteriously thunder in the distance, Kayla began to feel as if maybe she had a partial blame in the events taking place as she watched her colleague attempt to do the unthinkable.

"Kayla, get your ass down here and help us," yelled Meg.

Kayla heard the voice, but her limbs still couldn't move. She was angry, disgusted, and afraid at the same time. What happened to the compassion that a human being is supposed to possess? How could these people not imagine this being their daughter or sister. Then, it dawned on Kayla that neither of the two even had kids. They lacked the power of eternal love that creating life can give.

Even though Gabby had her faults, never in a million years did Kayla want to see her dead. She was even more appalled at the notion that they would seriously ask her to participate in something she had nothing to do with. Terrified by the two people that stood in front of her, Kayla prayed that God would give her the strength to make it out alive. Kayla's instincts told her to show no fear. These two weren't human; they were monsters, the devil's advocates. She continued to stand there as she watched these criminals attempt to cover up a murder.

"Whew, she packed on some pounds, huh Jared?"

"What do we do now?" he asked, not amused by her candid attitude.

"We drive to the cabins and dump her off in the woods. Meanwhile, the better question is…what do we do with Kayla?"

At that moment, Meg's voice crept into her mind and something overcame Kayla's spirit. She had an overwhelming feeling of strength take over her body. She walked over towards Meg and immediately grabbed her by the neck.

"I told you the next time you threatened me I would kill you, right?"

"Uhm, Kayla…will you calm down…just a little?" Jared pleaded, not knowing what to do.

"Now you listen to me," Kayla said, as she held Meg's neck a little tighter, "what you're going to do is make sure that money you put in my account is never traceable, and if anyone ever asks you do I know anything about Gabby, you tell them I haven't seen her since she left her position at the hospital."

"Kayla…please…you're choking me," pleaded Meg.

Kayla slowly eased her hold as Meg instantly stepped back and gasped for air. Kayla took one last look at Gabby and hoped that she was just unconscious and not dead. She knew she couldn't help Gabby, but she did want to give her a fighting chance.

"Before I go, I would suggest that you two hold off on the plastic, keep her head uncovered, wrap her up in a blanket, and put her in the backseat. That way, if you get pulled over by chance or come to a road block, she will look sleep in the back seat, opposed to dead in your trunk."

With that said, Kayla left seeming as if she had all the confidence in the world. Meg and Jared couldn't fathom how Kayla was able to take charge in a matter of seconds, but they began to unwrap Gabby as Kayla closed the door behind her. Once in her car, Kayla calmly drove off, but as soon as she was out of view, she burst into tears. She couldn't believe she just witnessed a murder by two highly decorated people of the community. Gabby had to have had damaging information on both Jared and Meg, since Meg was okay with Gabby being dead. Kayla was distraught that she was now involved in yet another case that would haunt her for life.

Kayla arrived home feeling overwhelmed and shaken by what had just took place. She wasn't ready to tell Bryan about what happened in fear of his reaction. Kayla was undecided if she should anonymously call the police and report Meg and Jared or allow them to destroy themselves. From what Kayla knew, Gabby was still married even after her affair with Raymond, so it would seem as if her husband would put out a missing person report at some point. What if Gabby had already told or gave her husband evidence of the dirt she had on Meg and Jared? What if Gabby's husband was in on the plot with Meg and Jared for money or revenge? The possibilities were endless as Kayla walked into the house and fell on the couch.

"Hey babe, are you okay?" Bryan asked, entering the living room.

"Everything is just overwhelming," Kayla admitted, beginning to cry.

"It's okay. I've never heard of anyone having perfect wedding arrangements," he said as he tried to console her, assuming she was referring to the wedding.

Kayla looked into his loving eyes and knew she was doing the right thing by keeping Bryan out of her mess. He was so passionate about her and Nicolas' well-being, and she didn't want her mistakes to interfere with their relationship. She kissed him and told him she was going upstairs to take the longest shower ever.

About 15 minutes had passed as Bryan was sitting down watching ESPN. The doorbell rang and Bryan assumed it was his cousins coming back from visiting his mom. He opened the door as Wayne stared in his face with a chilling look.

"Man, I heard yo bitch told my bitch that I killed her sister."

"Listen my nigga, we can talk about this calmly or get into some gangsta shit, but what you're not gonna do is disrespect my wife," Bryan threatened, closing the door behind him, so Kayla couldn't hear the argument.

"Oh Okay, so you tough now, huh?"

"Wayne, you've been my guy for a while. You're the best man in my wedding and will be the godfather of my first child. With that being said, I will protect my family by any means necessary and that means spending life in prison."

Wayne saw and heard the seriousness in Bryan's voice and took a step back. He looked around, put his hand over his mouth and then both hands on his head as if he wanted to say something, but couldn't find the words. He pulled out a black and mild, lit it, and began shifting his legs from side to side for a few minutes before speaking.

"I fucked up, dog," Wayne finally admitted.

"What do you mean?"

"I was at Justice's apartment that day."

"Oh fuck dude, are you serious? Tell me your kidding, bruh."

"It's not what you think though, Bryan, listen to me, man. After you told me you didn't want to add any outside girls to the mix, I took Justice on as my personal little project. Everything was cool, she was mad funny, hella sexy, one thing led to another, and we started fucking on a daily."

"Wayne, listen man, I know you do ya thang, but why would you start fucking this girl knowing you were already with her sister."

"That's the thing; I didn't even know they were sisters until that same morning. Justice told me she was having my baby. That's when I reminded her that I already had a girl and she was just my employee. She got all hysterical, she ended up snatching my phone, and she saw Jesse's picture on my main screen."

"Get the fuck outta here, dude."

"Man, I swear da' God that's how it happened. She started screaming, saying she was going to kill the baby and tell Jesse, and some mo shit. I asked her how did she even know that the baby was mine. Man, I tell you this bitch literally punched me in the face."

"Damn, so what did you do?"

"I didn't do too much of anything. I grabbed her by her face, threw her down against the counter, and walked out."

"Did you check to see if she was still breathing?"

"Man, hell yeah she was still breathing. She was crying on the floor and yelling and shit. The next thing I know, a few hours later, Jesse came running to me, talking about her sister is dead."

"So you never told her?"

"Hell no, man. That girl was still alive when I left that apartment. Somebody had to have come in after I did. Maybe she told them she was pregnant by me and they got jealous and killed her."

Although Wayne's story sounded convincing, Bryan just didn't know what to believe. Wayne could've made up the story because he needed someone in his corner, or he could've been telling the truth. Either way, Bryan knew that Kayla wasn't going to allow Jesse to come around and she probably didn't trust Wayne either. It was going to come down to helping save his boy or appeasing his wife.

Chapter 15

The big day had finally arrived and Kayla was vomiting in her bathroom from what she thought was nervousness. Bryan had stayed the night at his mom's house, so he wouldn't see Kayla 24 hours before the wedding. This was a plus for Kayla since she didn't want him to see her take the anxiety pills that Dr. Roberts gave her. She knew her reaction to them was risky, but she figured it would help with the vomiting. Through text messaging, Bryan explained that there wasn't anyway to find another best man on a short notice, so Wayne had to attend. Although Kayla was uneasy about Wayne's presence, she agreed to him being there minus his extra guest, Jesse.

The venue, coincidently chosen and paid for by Meg as Kayla's wedding gift, expected the bride to arrive by 9a.m. The wedding party and groom were supposed to arrive an hour later, get dressed in the designated dressing rooms, and meet the photographer for pre-wedding photos. Kayla was running behind, but she managed to arrive 15 minutes late as she explained and apologized to the venue host. The host explained that it was okay since the majority of the wedding party had arrived early with the exception of Meg, Meg's guest, and the groom.

Kayla thought it was odd that Bryan's family had arrived early, but he wasn't with them. She wasn't too stressed since he wasn't expected for the next 45 minutes, so she began to allow the venue's make-up artist and hairdresser to beautify her. Her bridesmaids had already taken a tour of the venue and reported to Kayla how beautiful the hallways were decorated in silver and gold trimmings, which were the colors of Kayla and Bryan's choice. With walls drenched in sheer white, gold, and silver drapes that matched the ceiling chandeliers, the wedding area was magnificently decorated with white roses that had golden sprinkles and golden petals to match their exquisite taste. The reception hall that was in an adjacent building was a mirror image of the wedding area. The wall behind the alter was made purely of massive vertical windows that led out to a beautiful swan lake.

"Did Bryan seem just as nervous as I am?" Kayla asked, breaking the ice in the dressing room.

"Bryan ended up leaving last night, so we really hadn't seen him since," answered Renee, one of the cousins.

"Is his mom here?" Kayla continued to question.

"Yes honey, she is in the dressing room getting ready. Don't you worry, everything is fine," said Evelyn, a different cousin as she glared at Renee.

Kayla could tell something was wrong, but they clearly weren't going to tell her. She watched as Evelyn made a hand signal for Renee to shut up, but Renee just brushed her off. Renee was holding something that she seemed to want to get out in the open.

"I don't know why you're looking at me like that, she's going to find out anyways," argued Renee.

"Find out what?" Kayla asked, now feeling her anxiety underway.

"Kayla, you look amazing, sweetie!" Bryan's mom interrupted, coming through the door and giving Kayla a hug, "I just peeked in on your very soon to be husband and he is looking so handsome. I am so happy for you two right now, I could cry," Irene added, beginning to cry.

"Oh, Ms. Irene, you're going to make me cry," admitted Kayla, tearing up. Kayla was happy that Bryan was there and not having second thoughts.

"Oh, sweetie, now don't you start crying, you're gonna make these hardworking ladies redo your beautiful makeup," said Irene.

"I think they added too much foundation to her face."

"Now Renee, if you don't have anything positive to say, sweetie, you can close your mouth," warned Ms. Irene to her niece.

"Thank you auntie, she's been negative since we got here. See, I told you, Kayla, everything was fine. You are apart of our family and we got your back as if you've always been apart of our family."

"Thank you ladies and I appreciate how you guys came through for me. I couldn't have asked for any more beautiful bridesmaids."

"So why didn't your best friends want to be your bridesmaids or do you even have friends?"

"Renee!"

"It's just a question you guys, calm down."

"No, it's okay, it's a fair question. Well, Bryan and Nicholas are actually my best friends. Between the hospital, family time, and events I have to attend for the hospital, I really don't have time to make friends. Rebecca, who I considered as a good friend, moved to Florida almost a year ago. I do also have a gay friend name Dexter, but I don't think any of the grooms would have been comfortable walking down the aisle with him, so Bryan and I decided to see if you guys would come and be our bridesmaids.

"That's right, Kayla, put her in her place real quick. The less female friends you have, the less drama you have to deal with."

"Well, I guess I can relate to that because I don't fool with these females out here, so they really don't like me either," added Renee.

"We wonder why," Evelyn said and laughed.

Kayla relaxed and the medicine she took earlier was really starting to take affect in her system. She began to laugh and converse with her new family members as they told her stories about Bryan's past. She wasn't sure if Bryan or his mom had told the ladies about the Ms. Jenson situation, so she made sure not to accidently slip up and mention it. She even started warming up to Renee as they continued to discover that they had ideas and opinions in common. Moments later, Kayla's mom walked in with a few of her own family members as everyone greeted one another. Kayla felt warm inside and happy that everything was turning out according to planned. Kayla always dreamed for her future of this bliss.

"Hello everyone," a familiar voice chimed, walking into the room.

"Meg!"

"Yes, Hun, you know I wouldn't miss your big event," she said, walking over to give Kayla a small hug.

What the fuck is she doing here, this Satanist is going to curse my fucking wedding, thought Kayla.

"Hello ladies, my name is Meg, I am Kayla's boss and close friend. This venue was actually my wedding gift to Kayla, so I hope you all are comfortable and pleased with the accommodations. It's definitely my pleasure to meet my favorite gal's family."

Kayla looked at Meg as if she saw the devil himself. It was just like Meg to make an awesome first impression and then try to roll your dead body in plastic if you crossed her. It was even clearer to Kayla how she was pulled into Meg's web of lies.

"Oh, Kayla, you are even more stunning than I imagined. I can't wait to show off your photos to our foundation members that couldn't attend."

"Yeah, uhm, Meg, can I see you in the hall for a brief minute?"

"Sure Hun, excuse me ladies, I promise I won't keep your beautiful bride long."

"Wow, I wish my boss was that nice," said one of the cousins as Kayla closed the door.

"So, how are you feeling bride-to-be?"

"Meg, cut the 'cookie cutter great boss' shit, okay? What are you doing here?"

"I have a front row seat to this glamorous event, so what do you mean?"

"Meg, seriously, why are you here?"

"Well, since you want to be like that, I'm here because I have no other option. I have to make sure everything looks ordinary and if we both play our cards right, we'll be out of this situation scot-free."

"I'm not in any situation, you and Jared demonic asses need to stay clear of me, do you understand?"

"Judge me not for ye may be doomed too, Kayla. You still have the money, right?"

"So."

"So, that means you're just as guilty as us. Stop acting as if you belong in Barbie's playhouse and not the pen. Besides, Gabby disappeared, so technically, we didn't kill her."

"What!"

"Hey, hey, hey, you keep your voice down."

"What do you mean she disappeared?"

"Jared and I left Gabby's body in the car about a mile down from the cabin in order to make sure there weren't any unexpected renters in the condo. Once we returned to the car, her body was missing."

"You have got to be kidding. How long did you leave her down there?"

"Long enough...we had to uhm...clean up some things."

"You guys went to have sex while there was a dead body in your car?"

"No one said we had sex."

"Your grin said it all. You two are fucking maniacs and you're screwed."

"He's worth every hard screw. That Italian dick is amazing! I'm sure you understand, I mean, you are marrying a black man."

"You won't be joking when you're doing twenty to life."

"Really, Kayla, and what's with the language lately? We left the windows in the car down, so a bear probably got her and besides, she's in a hundred miles of woods. She'll never make it out of there alive."

"A bear probably got her? That shit is unrealistic."

"If she makes it out alive, no one is going to believe her over us. Jared said he already got whatever so-called blackmail evidence she claimed she had against us, so everything is cool and now, we're technically not killers without a body."

It was at that point that Kayla knew Meg was completely insane. She had to be the dumbest woman around or the most egotistical to think she was in the clear. Kayla was lost for words as she stared at Meg as if she had two heads on her shoulders.

"Why are you looking at me that way? I thought you would be happy about the news since it was your idea not to bag her. At least the poor girl didn't suffocate."

"Now you listen here Meg. I am done playing you and Jared's little game. I'm going to give you back the money and I want out."

"Kayla, we need you back in here, dear. They're almost ready to start the pre-wedding ceremony pictures," said the stylist.

Kayla didn't say another word as she walked back into the room with a dark cloud over her head. She wasn't sure if Meg was telling the truth, lying in order to keep Kayla from talking, or maybe Meg just wanted to keep Kayla entangled in their twisted circle. Meg was one lunatic that she wished she hadn't ever met.

Trying to keep a beautiful smile while taking pictures, Kayla's mind couldn't help but to wonder. If Meg was telling the truth, how long was Gabby unconscious? Could Gabby have heard the conversation where Kayla actually helped to save her life? Did she hear the part where Kayla admitted to having the money in her bank account? Kayla wasn't sure about anything, but she was hoping that Meg was trying to scare her because if Gabby was still alive, she would literally control their lives.

An hour later, the ceremony was starting and Kayla was nervous as ever. Everyone in the wedding party was dressed and set up in the ceremony room, the guests were waiting and watching as the bridesmaids and groomsmen walked down the aisle in sync with the song "Spend My Life With You," and it was time for Kayla to walk out. The audience gasped as she walked out in a beautiful, soft white, shoulder-less dress with a diamond-studded center from her cleavage down to her waist and a flowing train. Bryan's eyes as he looked upon her with love and admiration. He grabbed her hand as the preacher began to talk and refer from the Bible. The preacher asked for the rings as Wayne came up to pass them to Bryan. He winked at Kayla, stood back into his position, and looked into the audience and gave the same wink. Kayla followed his glance to Jesse, who was sitting in the third row.

She focused back on Bryan who seemed unaware of what was going on. She warned Bryan not to have that bitch at her wedding. Now, in addition to Meg, she had two cursed whores at her wedding. She couldn't make a scene in the middle of the ceremony. She momentarily ignored the minor aggravation.

Once the wedding was over, the venue host immediately escorted the wedding party outside for pictures. The wedding was amazing and Kayla was in bliss with her new husband. They took some awesome shots, as Kayla temporarily had no cares in the world. Once the outside pictures were over, Kayla went back into the venue and headed toward the dressing room to go change into her reception dress. About halfway there, she saw Jesse walking down the hall.

"Hey, you weren't invited to my wedding and you need to leave now!"

"And you're going to make me in that dress," challenged Jesse.

"I wouldn't mess up a hair on my head for you. Security!" yelled Kayla.

Two women and a man quickly came from around the corner to see what was going on in the hall. Kayla explained that Jesse was an intruder and they immediately began to escort her out.

"I hope that all hell comes upon this wedding!" she yelled as they removed her from the building.

After Kayla was finished getting dressed, they escorted her and Bryan to the reception building where they announced the new Mr. and Mrs. Phillips. Kayla explained what happened with Jesse once they were sitting down ready to be served dinner.

"Kayla, you couldn't just leave it alone for today?"

"Bryan are you serious? This is our wedding and we don't need any bad spirits around."

"Really, because I know I've seen your boss fifty times already."

"She paid for the venue, Bryan."

"So, that doesn't mean she could have stopped the wedding."

"Look, I didn't have to knock out Meg in my house, so she isn't a threat."

"She's a threat if she got you shot at."

"I am not going to argue with you on our wedding day."

"I'ma go and get me a drink."

"Uhm, excuse me, Mr. Bryan Phillips?" asked a man in a gray suit.

"Yeah, that's me."

"Bryan Phillips, you've been served," the man said as he put a folder in Bryan's hand and quickly vanished.

"What is this?" asked Kayla, standing beside Bryan.

"Hell, I don't know, probably a contract deal from work that went wrong, shit, I'll open it later."

"No, that's probably something from Jackie," Renee confessed, peeking over Bryan's shoulder.

"What is she talking about and who is Jackie?" Kayla asked as she looked at Bryan while he glared at his cousin with disgust.

"Bryan has a 16-month-old baby that you don't know about with Jackie Jenson, Ms. Jenson's niece."

Bryan quickly grabbed Renee by the neck as other family members rushed over to her rescue.

"Payback is a bitch, huh Bryan? You married a dog!" she yelled as they escorted her out the building.

Kayla grabbed Bryan's hand and pulled him outside to a private area. He couldn't look Kayla in the face. He put his arm against the building and laid his head on it.

"Please tell me this is some made up bullshit, Bryan."

"Kayla, I swear I didn't know. My momma told me that some girl had been leaving her voicemails for my mom to call her. The next thing I know, I get a call from some attorney saying I'm about to get put on child support and I need to go take a DNA test."

"So you didn't think to discuss this with your wife before now? I had to find out word of mouth that we're still fucking dealing with the Jensons!"

"Kayla, I just found out yesterday and I don't even know if the baby is mine."

"So you went to see this Jackie bitch last night, huh?"

"I just wanted to see if the baby resembled me."

Kayla reached back and slapped him. "You went to go see your ex-girlfriend who is related to my arch enemy the night before our wedding!"

"I didn't go see her; I went to look at the baby."

"You didn't return to your mom's house that night, so what did you do, meet up with Jennie too and have a threesome?"

"Kayla, that's ridiculous. I know that Renee been filling ya' head up since she feels I'm the reason why her baby daddy went to jail and she had a miscarriage."

"Fuck Renee and her problems. I need to know what the fuck happened last night?"

"Nothing happened, Kayla. I asked Jackie why she waited so long to tell me that I could possibly be her baby's father. She said she didn't want Jennie to find out we use to fuck and the guy she was with turned out not to be the dad. She said I was the only other option."

"I'm fucking done, I'm getting this damn marriage annulled," she yelled, quickly walking off.

Bryan came from around the corner to grab her, but a crowd had already gathered outside in the front of the building surrounding a police car.

"What the hell is going on now?" Bryan asked his mother who was standing near the commotion.

"I don't know, baby, they escorted some woman out in handcuffs.

Kayla looked into the crowd and quickly recognized the woman they were putting into the back of the squad car. The officers were putting Meg in the back seat with her head hanging low. She had the exact same look on her face as Mr. Wright had the night he shot her.

"While you're judging me for my demons, you need to make sure you hold yourself accountable for yours," Bryan said, walking back into the building.

Kayla heard him, but her mind was scattered. Kayla knew by them arresting Meg that it had to have meant that they found Gabby dead or alive. She knew that Meg was a snake and would find some way to involve her in the plot. As Kayla stood there and watched the car drive Meg away, she watched her shortly, blissful moment drive away as well. Jesse's wish had come true; Kayla's wedding had quickly become an unholy matrimony from hell.

www.imadethebook.com

Be sure to check out previous editions

Partially Broken Never Destroyed I

Partially Broken Never Destroyed II: Mirror Mirror

Partially Broken Never Destroyed III: The Trilogy

Other books

The Experience of Life vs. Expert Advice

Unleashing Essential Oils: With Extra Beauty Tips

My Diet Your Diet We Diet

LINKS

Author Home Page
www.imadethebook.com

Amazon: Author Page
https://www.amazon.com/Nataisha-T.-Hill/e/B00KW25CH2/ref=ntt_dp_epwbk_0

Facebook Page https://m.facebook.com/taymadethebook/?ref=bookmarks

Twitter
https://twitter.com/AuthorTHill

Pinterest Account
https://www.pinterest.com/taisha005/